What readers are s

"This story could not have com... ....y

has love, joy, heartache and laughter. The remarkable courage,
strength and perseverance Ben and Norma show through this story is
a great life lesson. Many people can relate to this and gain insight
and strength from it. I also like that fact that we need to keep great
inspiring people alive, or that the story of great people can fade.
Thank you so much for sharing this story."

Alison

* * *

What an enchanting story! Disney should make a movie of this!

Christine

* * *

Loved it, so fun.
It was so lovely to sit and wrap myself up in a warm story. To see
love in action. I would have to limit myself to a set time, rush to get
things done, and then have some more time with the Frosst's.
You, my dear, have written a delightful story. An opportunity to
relax with characters that seem like good friends. It was lovely. I'm
looking forward to reading it again, wrapped in a soft blanket, ready
to feel warm from your words. Well done, Diane.

Kay

* * *

From the opening statement to the last summation, Diane had my
full attention. I loved how the story unfolded and kept me excited for
the next turn of events. She has masterfully shaped the story of
"Frosty the Snowman" into an enchanting composition I would
never have imagined in my wildest dreams. I loved it from beginning
to end. And, Yes, it made me cry!

Christine

* * *

This was an awesome story, Diane. I love how your books give us the "facts" behind the legend.
I can't wait to buy several copies!
Sheila

* * *

What a well-written touching sweet story. Your use of terrific dialogue and descriptive words drew so much emotion and tenderness. Thank you for such a sweet, touching story.
Karen

S*now Man

Diane Stringam Tolley

S*nowMan

Diane S*tringam T*olley

Summary: Despite his handicaps, Ben Frosst finds ways to serve the children in his community.

Cover Photo by Jodi Crisp
Cover design © 2015 by Kristi Pfeiffer
Edited by Caitlin Clark

For my family.
For your loyalty and your belief in me.
And for all my readers.
For your unfailing encouragement and enthusiasm.

Chapter One

"Ben?" There was a pause, then, a little louder, "John Benjamin Frosst, can you hear me?"

Ben moaned slightly and put a hand to his head.

"Ben?" Another, softer voice joined the first. "Ben, honey? It's Norma."

Ben turned his head toward the second voice. "Orma?" The voice was a mere whisper of sound.

"Yes, honey, it's me."

He reached out a tentative hand and felt it clutched by cold fingers. "Orma?" he said again, a little louder.

"Oh, Ben!" her voice broke and he could hear the soft sound of sobs.

He slowly reached with his other hand and touched her hair. "S'okay, hon." It was an effort to get the words out, but he tried again. "S'okay."

He felt her head tilt toward him.

He cleared his throat weakly. "S'okay."

"Ben, can you open your eyes?" the first voice was back. Ben wrinkled his forehead, trying to force a name into his mind. Jim –

Job . . . Rob. Yes, that was it – Rob.

He cracked an eyelid but the bright light stabbed so he jammed it shut. "S'bright," he mumbled. "Bright."

He heard the sound of something sliding and he again opened one dark eye a slit.

Someone had closed the blinds.

Ah, that was better. He opened the other eye slightly to see several shadows hovering above him. He opened wider and the shadows coalesced into metal stands with glass bottles dripping fluids into his veins. And people, standing on either side of the bed.

A woman in a starched white cap and uniform straightened away from him and nodded. Then disappeared on silent feet.

He closed his eyes again. "Where am I?" he croaked.

"Ben, you're in . . ." Norma's voice again broke.

"You're in the hospital, Ben," Rob said, slowly and clearly. "You were in an accident. Do you remember?"

Ben frowned heavily. An accident? Suddenly, he could see a road – dark and rain-slick – with oncoming lights that swerved across the center line. There was no time to get out of the way.

"Nodime," he said.

[2]

"What's that, buddy?"

Ben shook his head slightly, then moaned and put his free hand to his forehead. "Nodime."

There was silence in the room. Then, "Ben, we have some things we have to discuss with you."

Ben opened his eyes again and squinted, trying to focus on the doctor, who also happened to be his friend. "Disscussss?"

"Yes, Ben. I'm afraid I have bad news."

Ben felt a wave of blackness sweep over him and he closed his eyes.

"Ben. Ben!" The cold fingers gripping his one hand tightened. "Ben?"

Finally, he opened his eyes again. "Discuss?" he said, a little more clearly.

"Ben, I have some bad news."

"Bad," Ben said.

"Yes, my friend. Are you awake?"

"Ssorta."

"Close enough." Rob cleared his throat. "Ben, you were in an accident. A very bad accident with the bus. You're going to be all right, but you've . . . well . . . you've . . . lost your legs."

The last few words came out in a rush and Ben frowned and tried to concentrate on them. He could tell they were important, but they bounced freely around inside his skull and resisted all efforts to grasp them. He finally decided to try to fasten on just one. Ahh, he had it. Legs. Rob had said something strange about legs. "What about . . . legs?" he asked.

"Ben, listen carefully to me." Rob spoke a little more slowly. "You were in a bad accident. You've lost your legs."

Suddenly Rob's words seemed to pierce through into the fog inside Ben's head. "Legs? Lost?" The words were dragged out of him. He looked down at himself, lying on a narrow metal bed and covered to his chest with thick, gray, wool hospital blankets. He frowned and tried again, "Lost?"

"Yes, Ben. In the accident. Your lower legs were so badly damaged that we just couldn't save them. We had to . . . well, they're gone."

"Ben?" Norma spoke up again. "You're going to be all right, honey. We'll get through this together."

Ben turned toward her. She was hatless. Her blonde, normally smooth, exquisite hair was unpinned and hanging about her face, uncombed. Fine skin had darkened about her aqua-blue eyes and made them look sunken and ill. Her tall, slender, figure looked somehow shrunken.

"Normayoulookawful," he said slowly.

She ducked her head and caught her breath on a sob.

"S'okay, hon." He reached out uncertainly and patted the soft hair. "S'okay."

She released his hand and pulled out a soggy handkerchief. "Oh, Ben!" She scrubbed at eyes and nose.

Ben frowned. "Foot hurts."

"Ben. I told you . . ." Rob began.

Ben's eyes opened wide and he raised himself up on one elbow. "My foot hurts!" he shouted. Then he collapsed back onto his pillows. "Hurts!" he repeated, his eyes closing.

Rob sighed. "It's phantom pain, Ben," he said gently. "It's quite common among people who have lost limbs."

[5]

Ben was silent for a few moments. Then, his eyes opened once more and he struggled to focus. "The . . . kids," he said quietly. "They . . . make it?"

Rob glanced at Norma's tense, white face, then back at his friend. "Three of them have various injuries, but are expected to make full recoveries. The other six were only shaken up a bit."

Ben sighed and closed his eyes once more.

Rob touched Ben's arm. "I know you probably won't believe this right now, Ben, but you saved them all."

Ben opened one eye, then closed it and sighed again.

"No, really. If you had swerved even the tiniest bit, that truck would have hit the bus on the side where all of the kids were sitting and none of them would have made it. Because you, in the driver's seat, took the whole force of the collision, it . . . well . . . saved the boys."

"Got between them," Ben said quietly.

"What?"

"Got between them. Only had myself."

Rob looked at Norma and shrugged.

"I think he's trying to tell us that he deliberately steered the bus so that the truck would hit where he was sitting," Norma said.

"Put himself in harm's way." Rob nodded. "As I had guessed." He shook his head. "You're one in a million, Ben," he said, softly.

Ben sighed and turned his face away. He didn't speak again and soon slow, even breathing indicated that he had relapsed into slumber.

"I'd better be going, Norma," Rob whispered. "I want to check in on the Alberts boy before breakfast is served."

"Thank you, Rob." Norma got to her feet. She looked at her husband, lying so still in his narrow hospital bed. "Is he in . . . pain?"

Rob, too, looked over at the sleeping man. "I don't think so. We've kept him pretty sedated." He took a deep breath. "This hospital has just recently hired our first general anesthesiologist and he was able to keep your husband comfortable throughout the entire surgery. Now we have him on a course of opiates that should assure a continued degree of comfort."

Nora nodded and was silent for a moment. Then, "I know how hard you fought to save him, Rob. To save them all." She looked back at the doctor. "Thank you." she held out her hand.

[7]

Rob sighed and pressed the proffered hand briefly. "You're welcome," he said quietly. He shook his head and looked at her. "You know, Norma, there have been some marvelous breakthroughs in surgical procedures. Why only two years ago, in '38, I was privileged to witness an open-heart operation. Can you imagine that? Operating on a living, beating human heart! And it was successful! The surgeon there predicted that we'd see hundreds of lives saved as procedures became even more refined and improved." He sighed. "But vascular surgery simply hasn't advanced enough for me to restore the circulation in your husband's shredded and crushed legs. Those tiny veins and arteries were just too small." He shook his head again. "I feel as though I had failed."

"Rob, don't feel like that! You . . ."

But Rob was gone.

"You didn't fail!" Norma said, a little more quietly. "You didn't!" She sighed and looked down at her husband. "We'll get through this, you'll see!" She looked up and caught her breath on a sob. "Everything happens for a reason."

Chapter Two

Slow tears slipped from the corners of Ben's eyes and into his ears and hair.

Norma rubbed a hand across her brow and fought to contain her own tears. "You're alive, Ben," she said finally.

"This is living?" Ben demanded, holding out his arms and looking briefly down at himself. "Is that what you call it?"

Norma's lips quivered and she blinked her eyes rapidly. "Yes," she whispered finally. She looked at her husband. "You have to know that when they first brought you in that horrible evening t-two weeks ago . . . I . . ." she swallowed. "I thought you were . . . were . . ."

"Well maybe it would have been better if I had been!" Ben threw one arm across his eyes.

"Ben, don't say that!" Norma's voice had risen. She took a deep breath and tried again. "Ben, when they brought you in, I thought you were dead." She sighed softly. "My dear, even the emergency crew thought you were dead."

Ben lowered his arm and looked at his wife.

"But Rob wouldn't give up. He kept on trying and trying." She looked away. "He said you still had things to do." She took another breath. "He said that no friend of his, with your potential, was going to die at thirty!"

Ben rolled his eyes and looked toward the ceiling.

"And he was right, Ben," Norma went on. "He was right."

"I have things to do?" Ben sounded tired. "With my half-a-body?"

Norma nodded. "Yes, Ben. With your half-a-body," she said steadily.

He sighed. Then he turned his head and looked at her again. "I loved to run and play sports. I was going to organize the boys into a basketball league."

"We'll find something else for you to organize," Norma said firmly.

"And I loved to work at the factory."

"You can still work at the factory. The last time I checked, they had smooth cement floors. Just right for a wheelchair."

"And I loved being with the children."

"You can still be with the children."

[10]

He snorted. "Right. Maybe they could use me *as* the basketball."

Norma gasped out a laugh, then horrified, covered her mouth with one hand. "Sorry, dear."

Ben smiled. His first real smile in weeks. "That's all right. It's funny to me too." He was silent for a few minutes.

Norma got up and walked over to the window, looking outside on the wide, green park below them.

Finally, Ben sighed and scrubbed at his face with the crisply-starched sheet. "You're right. I can still do things. I'll just have to do them differently."

Norma turned back to him. "Everything happens for a reason."

"Well, I would much rather something *different* had happened."

"That's what we all wish when things don't go as we want."

Ben shrugged. Then nodded.

* * *

"I understand that they're quite common," Norma reached for Ben's hand. It felt hot and dry. "These infections, I mean."

Ben smiled weakly. "I feel like a frail little kitten. Could you please pass me that glass of water?"

Norma handed it to him. "Well, until we get you healed, you *are* frail. But it's only temporary."

"But this is the third time!" Ben paused to drink thirstily. "The third infection in . . . how long have I been here?"

"Just over two months."

"Two months." Ben shook his head. "Our lives have been on hold for two months."

"No, they haven't."

"Well, what do you call it, dear? Accomplishing great and important things?"

"That's exactly what I call it," Norma said, stoutly. "You *have* been accomplishing great and important things."

"Yeah. Learning to do things that the average baby can do when they are a few months old."

Norma smiled slightly. "We are all given challenges, Ben. Some greater than others."

"Who would have thought my challenge would be learning to sit up, turn over and get myself around. At thirty!"

"But at least you *can* do all of those things."

Ben relaxed back on his pillow and was silent for a moment. "Do you know what my dream was, Norma?"

Norma shook her head.

"It was you and children. Lots of children." He sighed. "Our home, the factory and serving in the community." He snorted softly. "Did I tell you that I had even been approached to run for mayor?"

"Oh, you'd make a fine mayor."

"*Would have.*"

"Why do you say that?"

"Honestly, Norma, are you looking at the same man I'm looking at?"

"I think so." She tipped her head to one side. "Dark hair, black eyes, strong chin." She tweaked the tip of Ben's nose. "Cute, button nose."

Ben self-consciously put his hand up to cover it.

Norma laughed, pulled his hand away and went on. "Good teeth, strong arms and very intelligent brain." She nodded. "Yes, I think we're both looking at the same man. And I think he would make a fine mayor. There's nothing in the town's bylaws that say a mayor actually has to 'run' for office."

Ben laughed, a short, quick burst of sound. Then he arched one eyebrow. "Very intelligent?"

"Very, very."

He smiled and then sighed. "Well, I wish I could just kick these wretched infections."

"Don't worry, they are a part of healing," another voice said.

"Rob! How nice to see you!" Norma extended her hand.

Rob shook it briefly and moved closer to Ben. "Still hot and dry, old man?"

Ben shrugged. "Can't seem to get enough to drink. And one minute I'm boiling hot. The next, freezing."

"Well, let's have a look at things, shall we?" Rob folded back the covers on Ben's bed and deftly removed the bandage covering the stump of one leg. "Hmmm . . ."

Norma walked around to the far side of the bed and reached for her husband's hand. "What is it, Doctor?"

"Well, the one leg is healing nicely. But I'm not happy with this one." He leaned back and peered into Ben's face. "You are flushed with fever, Ben. We need to get fluids into you and I think I'll start another course of sulfa."

Ben sighed. "Will it work this time?"

"It worked last time. But that was a month ago."

"Okay, Doc, have it your way." Ben shrugged. "But I should think that once the germs were beat, they'd be gentlemen and stay beat."

Rob smiled. "But they aren't gentlemen, Ben. I thought you knew that."

"Well, I do now." Ben sighed. "I do wish I could end this," he said softly. "I'm so tired of feeling lousy."

"We'll get the job done." Rob rewrapped the bandage. "I'll send the nurse in with your medication."

"Thanks, Rob." He held out his hand. "I really do appreciate everything you've done for me."

Rob looked at his friend, lying in his hospital bed, legless and burning up with fever. He sighed as he took the dry hand and gave it a squeeze. "I do wish I could do more, Ben. I surely do." He straightened. "But I've been discussing your case with some colleagues of mine and we've decided that the best thing for you is to start on a course of exercise."

"Doc, I can hardly lift my head!'

"Oh, we'll get past this latest infection. And then I think we'll rig some things up in here and start taking you down to the exercise room once a day."

Ben grinned crookedly. "You're the doc, Doc."

* * *

Ben sat at the window, looking out on the snow-covered park below. A slow tear worked its way down one cheek. "First snow of the season," he told himself quietly. "Look at the children out playing."

"I saw them as I came in."

He glanced up in surprise and brushed self-consciously at his face.

Norma was shaking glistening flakes off her coat and appeared not to notice. She pulled the warm fur off and laid it across the chair beside the narrow hospital bed. "They look like they're having fun!"

"They've . . . ." His voice faltered. Ben cleared his throat and tried again. "They've been having a snowball fight." He leaned his face against the cold pane and pointed. "Young Daniel has everyone organized." Then, with forced cheerfulness, "Look at all of the fortifications and blinds he's come up with!"

[16]

Norma smiled. "He would. He's pretty much the leader." She looked at her husband, "As you taught him."

Ben snorted, pushed his wheelchair back abruptly from the window and turned to look at his wife. "In my past life." He pushed the wheels of his chair, propelling himself smoothly across the room.

Norma watched him for a moment. Softly, she said, "Rob says he's very pleased with your continued improvement."

Ben said nothing. He moved his chair close to the bed and carefully set the locks. Then he reached for a bar hanging on two chains above him and used it to maneuver himself over and onto the mattress.

Norma watched him carefully.

When he was nestled once more among the sheets and pillows, she shook her head. "You've really made remarkable progress in four months."

"Yeah. I can swing my little half-a-body around like I'm on a jungle gym!" Ben said bitterly. "Regular Tarzan!"

Norma's blue eyes filled with tears.

He sighed. "I'm sorry, hon," he said more softly. "I'm just so darn . . ." He looked at her and she was surprised to see tears pooling in the beloved, black eyes.

"Ben? What's the matter?" Norma moved to the bed and reached for his hand.

Ben shook his head and brushed impatiently at his eyes. "It's nothing. It's just . . . I get so . . . angr-frustrated sometimes." He jumbled one word into another.

"It's totally understandable, Ben." Norma smoothed his hair. "Totally understandable."

He laid his head back against the pillows. "What am I going to do with my wreck of a life, Norma?" He looked at her. "How much more are we expected to take?"

"Ben, you're scaring me."

"What does one do when they're confronted with the inescapable? The horrifying and inescapable?"

Norma studied him for a moment, then sat back. "One goes on."

Ben snorted faintly. "Go on," he repeated.

She nodded uncertainly, frowning at his tone.

He took a deep breath, tears gathering in his eyes once more. "Because it's even more of a wreck that you can possibly imagine."

Something in his voice made her move closer. "Ben?"

He looked away, towards the corner of the room. "Rob gave me some more bad news, hon. I insisted that he let me tell you."

"More?" Norma's face whitened. "But you've been doing so well! You've beat the depression and ..."

She sank into the chair and reached out a hand to clasp cold fingers around her husband's warm ones. "How can there be more?" she asked, faintly.

Ben kept his eyes averted, gathering courage. "Rob says ... that there is no way we can ever have children."

Norma stared at him, her mouth hanging open slightly.

"Norma, honey, my ... they're ... I can't ... give you children." A tear trickled down the unshaven cheek. Ben threw his arm across his face and his chest heaved.

"Ever?" Norma was struggling to understand this latest blow. She put her other hand on his arm and shook it slightly. "Ever?" she repeated.

Ben lowered his arm. "Ever."

"Oh, Ben!" Norma struggled to her feet and teetered uncertainly for a moment. Then she slid onto the bed beside her husband.

He wrapped his arms around her and let her sob against his chest, his own tears making wet patches in her soft hair.

Sometime later, after the storm had passed, they stayed where they were. Silently coming to grips with this new challenge. Finally, Ben took a deep breath.

Norma sat up and looked at him.

"I've got to get out of here, hon," he said gently. "I've got to figure out what to do and I can't do it from this bed!"

"Well, Rob . . ."

"I don't care what Rob says. I've got to get on with whatever is left for me!" He looked at Norma. "Before we lose everything."

Norma nodded. "I'll go and get him."

* * *

Rob wasn't in the hospital. It was the next day before they managed to track him down and get him to Ben's room.

Ben looked at him. "I need to go home, Rob."

"Well, I don't see a problem."

[20]

"Really?" Ben said. "I thought you wanted to keep me here for at least another month!"

Rob shook his head. "No, you've made such progress in the past two that I don't have any trouble with having you continue on at home." He frowned at Ben sternly. "Provided you do continue . . . at home."

Ben smiled slightly. "I've already been talking to the members of my medical team. Everything's arranged."

"Well, you really have been making remarkable progress. I can't think of a single case in all my years of practice where someone's been through what you have and overcome it as well."

Ben grasped Norma's hand. "I've had help."

Rob smiled. "As long as it continues, you'll do just fine."

"It will," Norma tightened her fingers around her husband's.

"Good." Rob grinned at her. "I wish that all of my patients had your steadfast support."

"Well, we still have challenges to overcome." Ben looked at Norma. He sighed, "Big ones."

"But we'll do it," Norma finished.

"Well, I'll see to the paperwork and you should be out of here tomorrow or the next day."

Ben offered his free hand. "Thanks, friend."

Rob smiled, tiredly. "You're welcome." He left the room.

Norma smiled and smoothed Ben's hair. "It will be so nice to have you home, dear."

Ben looked around the small, bare, institutional room, softened only slightly by the addition of cards and flowers. "I won't miss this place, I can tell you." He shivered slightly. "There are too many . . . memories."

Norma got to her feet. "Let's start getting you packed."

* * *

The next morning, following tearful partings from the attentive staff that Ben had gotten to know so well, and cautions about possible setbacks, Ben and Norma were finally sitting in their car, Norma in the driver's seat.

Ben looked across at his wife. "We'll have to hire a driver."

Norma reached across and gripped his hands. "Lots of things to let future Ben and Norma worry about. Let's just get you home."

"Home." Ben smiled.

[22]

Chapter Three

"He's really made a remarkable recovery, Rob," Norma said.

"Physically, yes. But I'm a bit concerned about his mental and emotional health right now."

Norma stared at him. "You think he's . . ."

"Let's just say I wouldn't be doing my job if I didn't try to see the whole picture."

"Ah."

"We both know what a blow it has been for him to be so limited physically."

"Yes. To go from one who has been so active to someone who is not." Norma bit her lip.

Rob watched her for a moment. Then he nodded. "It takes its toll," he said gently. "On both of you."

Norma looked around at the fine furnishings and appointments in her elegant front room. "It's funny." she waved a hand. "We have so much that is exactly the same."

"Only the most important things have changed."

Norma nodded. "*The* most important." She rubbed her fingers across her smooth brow. "Ben has discovered that he can pretty

[23]

much keep up with work from his office here. Within a week of coming home, he had a telephone line connected directly to the factory. With that, it's almost like he's actually there. And he has several aides who run paperwork back and forth. I mean, it's not like it was, but over the past month we've seen the results and it's working." She frowned. "It's good that he has things in place because now, with all of this talk of the United States getting into the war, the orders to the plant have doubled."

Rob nodded. "All of that is very good news and the timing, for Ben, at least, couldn't be better. Getting back to work and keeping busy is probably the best thing that he could have done for himself." He looked at the tense woman seated across from him, slender fingers clutched together in her lap.

"But I'm talking about his . . . your . . . both of you . . . your relationship."

"Oh."

Rob took a deep breath. "I know what a blow it must have been," he said. "The initial accident."

Norma was silent.

"And Ben's loss of mobility." Rob looked at Norma. "And then to find out about your . . . children."

Norma put a hand to her quivering lips as her blue eyes filled with tears. "That is the hardest of all for him," she whispered, finally. "He loves children so much!"

Rob nodded. "I know. The whole town knows." He shrugged. "Let's face it, Norma, if he didn't love children so much, he wouldn't be in the mess he's in right now."

Norma nodded and looked away, tears starting to slide down her smooth cheeks. "He was so excited to take all of his scouts on that camping trip. They had been planning it for months."

Rob smiled. "I know. My neighbour's boy, Trent, had made his father take him shopping for the latest in outdoor gear. It had to be just like in the movies. Canteen, bedroll. The works."

Norma nodded, dabbing at her eyes. "He had the top of that poor old bus loaded."

"And the inside loaded with nine eager, little campers."

"It was the first time for most of them." Norma dabbed at her eyes again and blew her nose. "Excuse me." She tucked her handkerchief into her sleeve and leaned back in her chair. "When he took over the troop just after we were married . . ."

"You mean when he created the group just after you were married."

Norma smiled slightly. "Yes. He thought it was such a good program for training young men."

Rob nodded.

"But now . . ." Norma shrugged her shoulders.

"His assistant is trying to keep things going, but he's having a bit of a struggle."

Norma shrugged. "I know exactly what the problem is. He's not Ben." She sighed. "How he wishes he was with them." She looked at Rob. "He puts up a strong front, but I know what's going on in his heart. How he longs for children!"

Rob nodded again. "And we're back to my initial concern. I'm worried about Ben's emotional health."

Norma took a deep breath. "What can we do, Doctor? We've talked about his going back – mixing with the young people again. We've even talked about trying for children of our own through adoption. He always talks like he is excited and enthused, but I just don't know."

Rob was silent for a moment. "Actually, that was going to be my suggestion. Adoption."

"Well, we have discussed it." She sighed. "Several times."

Rob glanced at his pocket watch and stood up. "I have to be going. Rounds."

"Of course, Rob." Norma got to her feet. "I'll walk you to the door."

"Thanks."

They paused in the doorway.

"We got sidetracked from talking about your relationship, Norma."

"We're actually doing all right, Rob. Ben is very careful of me, but then, he always was. In fact, I think that this accident has actually improved our relationship in some ways."

"How so?"

"Well, you know Ben's father, what a sportsman he was."

"Yes."

"Gone all of the time on hunting trips or to sporting events. His wife and sons hardly saw him."

"I always thought Ben's mother was a saint."

Norma smiled. "As did I. Sadly, he would never take any of his boys. Even when they got old enough that they could have really benefited from the time together."

"Between you and me, his father's accident was more of a blessing than a burden." Rob spoke quietly.

"Well, let's just say that his family grieved. But they didn't miss him."

"Hard to miss someone who was never there."

Norma nodded. "The thing is that Ben was starting to get interested in the same things when he wasn't out with his scouts. Hunting. Sporting events." She shrugged. "Almost as though he was trying to make up for all that he thought he lost."

Rob shook his head. "Oh, the things our children learn from us."

"But my point is that he simply can't make any more hunting trips. And he still hasn't hired a driver to take him around so he's stuck with me."

Rob smiled. "That's tough to take!"

[28]

Norma smiled. "So I get Ben to myself whenever he's not working. And that's a very good thing."

Rob smiled, then stuck out his hand. "I'll be off. Let Ben know I was here and tell him what we talked about."

"I will," Norma promised.

* * *

"So he's worried about our relationship and my emotional health, is he?" Ben forked another bite of roast beef into his mouth.

Norma picked up her knife and started cutting the slice of tender beef on her plate. "Missy does this so well. I don't even need to use a knife." She looked up and saw Ben's eyes on her. "Oh. Yes. Well, we spent several minutes discussing it. He's worried that you are missing your scout troop."

Ben snorted softly. "Well, that I am. But it's only temporary." He grinned. "I have some news for you." He stabbed a pickle and waved it in the air. "I've been thinking and talking it over with Reed and we've decided that I can do their training and in-town stuff and Reed could take them when they do their camping and outdoor stuff." He looked around. "Heaven knows we have enough rooms in this great barn of a house. We can find some place suitable to meet."

[29]

Norma smiled, blue eyes shining. "Oh, Ben, that sounds really good!"

Ben grinned. "Better than good." He sighed and leaned back in his wheelchair. "But I'd be lying if I said that I'm not teeth-gnashingly jealous that I have to miss any future camps."

He glanced out the window. "I was going to take them all on a winter camp. It's the most fun of all!"

Norma shuddered. "I leave that to you. Summer camping, I can handle, but going out in the snow? Digging out a suitable spot? Building fires? Staying warm? Ugh!" She smiled at her husband. "Give me a warm blanket, a crackling fire and a good book and I'm happy camping in my front room!"

"Chicken!" Ben grinned at her.

"Completely, happily so."

He turned back to the window. "Winter is going to be the hardest." He sighed. "It's my favourite time." He shook his head. "I do miss going out in the snow. There must be another foot of the stuff since yesterday!"

Norma followed his gaze and nodded. "It's so beautiful! Look at the pines. Their boughs are so loaded that they look as though they're going to break off!"

Ben sighed again.

Just then, someone knocked at the front door and they both heard Missy go to answer it. "Of course." Her voice reached them faintly. "Please step inside."

The door closed.

Ben and Norma frowned at each other. *Are we expecting anyone?* Ben mouthed to his wife.

Norma shook her head.

The two of them turned toward the doorway.

Missy, dressed in her usual starched black dress and snowy apron paused just inside. "Master Ben, Mistress Norma, there are some gentlemen to see you." She brushed a hand over her immaculate, gray-streaked hair. "*Young* gentlemen." She nodded and disappeared.

"Well!" Ben pushed his chair from the table. Spinning around, he moved smoothly across the gleaming floorboards and out into the wide hall.

[31]

Norma followed closely.

On the large front carpet, two young boys stood, soft caps in their hands. Both were rosy-cheeked from the crisp outside air and smelled strongly of the fresh outdoors.

Ben smiled happily and rolled forward. "Well, if it isn't my dear friends, the Bering brothers!" He offered his hand. "Daniel! How nice to see you, son!"

The tallest boy, red-haired, fourteen-year-old Daniel, grasped the proffered hand and ducked his head. "Nice to see you, sir." He glanced at Norma. "Ma'am."

"Hello, Teddy! You keeping your elder brother in line?" Ben shook hands with the smaller boy, eight-year-old Teddy, who looked up at his older brother adoringly through white-blond curls.

"He don't need me to do that, sir," Teddy said, proudly.

Daniel smiled and prodded his younger brother with an elbow. "He's teasing, you dope!" he whispered loudly.

"Oh."

Ben grinned. "What can we do for you two young men?"

Daniel twisted his hat between his hands. "Well . . . we . . . that is . . ." he started.

[32]

"We want you to come outside!" Teddy's voice was loud in the quiet hall.

Ben went still. "I don't know if you boys understand . . ." he said.

"We've . . ." Daniel began.

But Teddy eagerly interrupted. "We made you a sleigh!"

Ben stared at him. "Sleigh?"

"Yeah. Daniel was studying your wheelchair and looking at the s-s-sup . . ."

"Support system." Daniel supplied.

"Yeah, that." Teddy grinned. "And he said he could make something the same, but for the snow."

Daniel's rosy cheeks turned redder still.

Ben turned to the older boy. "Daniel, is this true?"

Daniel nodded. "Yes sir."

Ben laughed happily and slapped his hands down on the arms of his chair. "Well, we'll just have to have a look at this marvelous new invention! Missy!"

The little woman bustled in from the kitchen, drying her hands on a spotless, white towel. "Yes, Master Ben?"

"Could you please bring me my heaviest coat?"

[33]

Missy looked at Ben uncertainly. "Oh, Master Ben, are you sure?"

"More than sure." Ben nodded.

The woman glanced at Norma.

"Go ahead, Missy." Norma smiled. "And bring me mine as well, if you don't mind."

"And boots too!" Teddy called out after the retreating form. "For . . .," his face reddened and he looked up at Ben, his small face a picture of embarrassment.

Ben smiled and gave the young boy a little punch in the arm. "Don't worry about it, Teddy. Just think. I'll never have to hunt for shoes again!"

Both boys laughed and Teddy looked relieved.

Soon, Ben and Norma were bundled up in thick felt and fur.

Ben rubbed gloved hands together. "Okay, boys, let's see this great invention!" He rolled his chair to the door and Daniel swung it wide. "Oh!" he said.

Pulled up on the step was a small, wooden sleigh. The back had been raised and some straps and several layers of padding had been added.

"So this is my chariot!" Ben rolled his chair close and looked the sleigh over. "Looks pretty good, boys."

Both boys beamed and leaned forward eagerly, pointing out safety and comfort features.

"Well, I'm convinced." Ben grinned. "Let's see if we can fit me in there with all of those toasty blankets!"

The two boys each took one of Ben's arms over their shoulders, lifting him carefully. Then they slid him down into the sleigh. Soon, Ben was strapped and wrapped, ready for his first adventure in the snow. It was all accomplished with a minimum amount of fuss.

Norma pushed the now-empty chair back inside the house and pulled the door shut.

"Alright, team. Let's go!" Ben shouted happily.

"Just one more thing, sir." Daniel walked over to the bench beside the front door and retrieved a small box. "There's just the final touch." He opened the box and drew out a battered, silk top hat.

The brim had certainly seen better days, and was stained and faded. Someone had obviously tried to cover the discoloration with boot black, but with marginal success.

The top still struggled mightily to stand up, but years of abuse and ill-treatment had weakened the stiffening. It sagged slightly to the right. And into the stained and discoloured hatband, someone had shoved an ancient corncob pipe.

Daniel carefully inspected the placement of the pipe, then smoothed the hat tenderly and reached out to set it on Ben's head.

"Whoa!" Ben said, laughing. "Do you know where this has been?"

Daniel looked down at the hat fondly. "Mostly in my basement. It was my Grandpa's and Teddy and I have played with it since we were little."

"This belonged to your Grampa?"

The boys nodded eagerly. "It was his best 'going-about-town' hat," Teddy told him. "And his best pipe."

Daniel broke in, "So we decided that if we were going to take you around town, you needed to wear it."

"Well, in that case, put it on." Ben grinned. "I can see a trip about town won't be the same without it!"

Daniel placed it carefully on Ben's head.

[36]

Ben pushed it to a jaunty angle and leaned back in his sleigh. "Okay, team. I'm ready!"

The two boys picked up the loop of rope attached to the front of the sleigh and stepped inside it, pulling it to their waists.

They weren't an evenly matched team, Daniel being so much taller than his little brother, but they were enthusiastic. They leaned into the rope and the sleigh began to move.

"Here we go!" Teddy cried out.

They started out across the snowy lawn at a lope. If it hadn't been for the straps holding him firmly, Ben would have been pitched out the back. "Hey!" he shouted and clapped a hand to his hat.

Daniel glanced back and, seeing Ben's laughing face, he turned to his brother. "C'mon, Teddy! Let's give Mr. Frosst a real ride!"

The two of them, with Norma laughingly bringing up the rear, doubled their pace.

They flew past homes and yards and townspeople.

Astonished faces gaped at them and Ben called out greetings as they went.

Finally, they reached the town square where a group of children had gathered and were in the midst of a giant snowball fight.

"Oh, let's get in on that!" Daniel said excitedly.

Norma moved closer. "Wait a minute. Shouldn't you . . .?" But her words were lost on the boys.

Already, they had pulled the sleigh to the edge of the crowd. "We're here to play!" Daniel shouted loudly.

The other children turned to look at him then noticed Ben, red-cheeked and happy, sitting in the sleigh. Suddenly the air was filled with their excited cries. "Mr. Frosst! Mr. Frosst!" They clustered around the sleigh, small, mittened hands reaching out to touch or pat him.

Ben grinned at all of them and shook hands with as many as he could reach.

"Oh, Mr. Frosst, we've missed you!" one young girl said.

"Well, I'm here now. So whose team am I on?"

Everyone shrieked and scattered.

The two boys pulled Ben behind one of the mounds of snow that served as a blind. Then kept him amply supplied with snow as he threw missile after missile toward the opposing team. He proved to be quite proficient, even from his enforced sitting position.

Finally, just as the sun was touching the tip of the United Church steeple on the west side of the square, the children decided that they'd had enough. Breathing heavily, Daniel pulled Ben's sleigh to the edge of the square and sat down in the snow. "Whew!" he said. "That was fun!"

Ben smiled at the tall boy. "More fun than I've had for . . . about five months."

Daniel looked up at Ben's rosy cheeks and wide smile. "Really?"

"Well, since June."

"Oh, right," Daniel said, looking slightly uncomfortable. "Wasn't thinking." He got to his feet. "Teddy! Come on. It's time to take Mr. Frosst home!"

The smaller boy appeared and the two of them started back toward Ben and Norma's home at a significantly slower pace than before.

Several people stopped them, greeting Ben with affection. "Ben! Good to see you up and about!"

"Ben! You're looking well!"

"Ben! Out with the kids again! So who won?"

There was much talk and laughter as the boys made their way along, finally pulling to a stop at Ben's front door.

Daniel started undoing straps. "We'll help you into your chair again, Mr. Frosst."

Norma retrieved the chair and the three of them soon had Ben safely back inside.

He held out his hand to the boys. "Thank you again, boys. It really was one of the best experiences of my life!"

The boys shook his hand, smiled and left.

"Well," Ben sighed, happily. "That's a bit more like it!"

Chapter Four

Over the next two weeks, the sight of Ben in his borrowed top hat – with pipe – being pulled by one or more boys was common on the streets of the village. Almost as common as seeing him, almost invisible amidst a hail of snowballs, giving as good as he got.

"Gee, Mr. Frosst, you are just too good," one of the younger players lamented as he wiped snow from his eyes. "No one can hit you!"

Ben laughed and spread his arms wide. "Come on, Harry. Try!"

Harry grinned and threw a perfect snowball. That sailed out and over his victim's head. The small boy looked up into the air, his face a perfect picture of chagrin. "Rats!"

Ben laughed. "Okay, you can't blame that one on me!"

Harry, face intent, started rolling another.

"I think you'd better get me out of here," Ben whispered loudly to Daniel.

The older boy laughed and grabbed the rope.

* * *

That evening, just before dinner, Norma stepped out onto the cleanly-swept front sidewalk. "Ben, what are you doing? Honey, it's freezing out here!"

From the middle of the walk, Ben laughed. "I'm dressed," he said. He held up a mittened hand, then smacked a broom against the brickwork, dislodging a clump of snow. "I just thought I would come out here and sweep the snow away."

"Ben, that's what we pay the servants for."

"But it's more fun to do it yourself." Ben grinned.

Norma smiled. "Ah. And it's much easier to roll a chair on a clean surface."

Ben looked at her, his grin widening. "You're smart. Someone should marry you!"

"Ben!" Norma said, slapping his arm playfully.

Ben's grin widened as he pulled his wife into his lap. "Oh, that's right." He nuzzled her ear. "Someone already did."

"Ben! You'll hurt yourself!"

"Nonsense. You don't weigh very much!"

Norma laughed and relaxed against him. She looked around. "It is beautiful out here, isn't it?"

[42]

The red brick of their beautiful two-story house made a lovely contrast to the window boxes, balconies and roof, piled high with snow. Tall pines leaned in close, their boughs also heavy with soft, white stuff.

The scene was peaceful. Serene.

Ben sighed. "It's my favourite spot on earth," he said, simply. "At my favourite time of the year."

Norma nodded. Then looked at him. "It is for me, too. As long as you're here."

Ben laughed. "Really? You don't think I'm the one short, sour note in the whole concerto?"

Norma laughed. "Well . . ." she narrowed her eyes and studied him. "Maybe."

"Hey!"

She laughed again and kissed him tenderly. "Sour or not, it's the one note I couldn't get along without." She slid off his lap. "But I'm supposed to call you in for dinner."

"Mmm, food. I'll be right in as soon as I finish up."

"Okay. But don't take too long or you'll have to face the wrath of Missy." She started back into the house.

[43]

Ben grinned after her. "I won't." He moved his chair further down the walk, reset the brake, swept a few feet, then moved again and repeated the whole operation.

In a few minutes, he had reached the far end.

"There!" He surveyed his work proudly. "Not bad for half-a-guy!" A red ball appeared, rolling slowly until it bumped into Ben's wheelchair. "Well, what do we have here?"

"Sorry, Mr. Frosst," a young boy's voice rang on the clear air. "It's my ball." Teddy Bering appeared, followed closely by his older brother.

"Sorry about that, Mr. Frosst," Daniel echoed. "Teddy was kicking it down the street. He's getting anxious for the snow to melt so he can get out into the field.

"Yeah," Teddy sighed. "I'm getting tired of waiting."

Ben laughed. "It's still more than a month to Christmas, son. You've got quite a wait."

"I know." Teddy sighed again.

Ben smiled and, using his broom, gave the ball a smack, making it sail toward the two boys.

Daniel caught it easily.

Ben grinned at him, then turned back to Teddy. "So spring is your favourite time, eh?"

"Yeah." The small boy nodded enthusiastically. "I mean, it's lots of fun having snowball fights and all . . ."

"But only the rich kids can afford skates and stuff to play hockey," Daniel went on. "The rest of us have to . . . make do."

Ben studied the two brothers quietly. "No hockey, eh?"

Daniel shrugged. "We're used to it. We don't have a lot of time to play anyway."

"Because you spend so much of it pulling me around." Ben grinned at him.

The boys smiled back. "We like doing that, Mr. Frosst," Teddy said. "It's fun!"

"But you should probably be spending the time playing with the other kids."

"Naw. We'd rather spend time with you." Daniel glanced up at the darkening sky. "We'd better hurry, Ted. Mom will be wondering where we are."

"Okay." Teddy looked at Ben. "Bye, Mr. Frosst!" He bumped into his brother as both of them turned to go and knocked the ball out of his hands.

It rolled back toward Ben. "Hey, don't forget your ball!" Ben gave it another whack with his broom.

Teddy caught it this time. "Thanks, Mr. Frosst!" The two boys disappeared down the street.

Ben turned his broom over in his hands, studying it. Finally, he turned and pushed himself back toward the door of his home.

* * *

A few minutes later, he was facing his wife over the snowy cloth, fine china and heavy silverware of their dinner table.

Ben nodded his thanks as Missy finished ladling aromatic soup into his bowl and disappeared into the kitchen. He turned to Norma. "Did you know that there are lots of kids in the village who can't afford equipment to play winter sports?"

Norma frowned. "Really? I hadn't even thought about it."

"I hadn't, either." Ben frowned. "Shame on me."

Norma made a face. "Don't blame yourself, honey. How could you have known?"

[46]

"Well, I spend enough time with the kids, you'd think I would have noticed that some of them were being excluded because they couldn't afford proper equipment."

"But have you been to watch their hockey games?"

Ben shrugged. "Not lately."

"Well, there you go, then."

He sat silently for a few moments, drumming the fingers of one hand on the polished table.

"I know that look." Norma smiled. "What are you thinking?"

Ben looked across the table at her. "I'm thinking I need to do something about it."

"Yes. But what?"

"Well, I could simply go out and buy everyone the skates and equipment they need to participate," he said slowly. "But I suspect that would simply create a different set of problems."

"So what do you suggest?"

"I don't know. Maybe a game that takes equipment that everyone already has?" Ben's glance strayed over to the wall.

"What kind of game is that?" Norma's eyes were on her bowl as she scooped up another mouthful of soup.

[47]

"I don't . . . maybe a new game?" Ben started to grin.

Norma stared at him. "You've lost me."

He glanced again toward the wall.

This time, Norma followed his gaze and noticed the propped broom. "Ben! Why did you bring that dirty thing in here?"

Ben laughed. "It got me thinking."

"A broom." Norma raised one eyebrow and stared at her husband.

"A broom," Ben repeated.

"Go on."

"Well, I had just finished sweeping and was out there at the end of the walk when the Bering boys came past. Teddy was kicking a ball, impatient for spring so he could get out into the field and play." Ben smiled. "I hit the ball with my broom."

Norma frowned. "And . . .?"

"Daniel caught it. Then they did some apologizing for bothering me. And that's when Daniel told me that they couldn't afford to play sports with the 'richer' kids in town."

"And that's when you got your idea."

"Yeah." Ben grinned.

Norma sighed. "And your idea is . . .?"

"Broomball," Ben said.

"Broomball?"

"Yeah."

"I don't think I've ever heard of it." Norma frowned thoughtfully.

"It's a real game. I saw some kids playing it over at Connors Hill a couple of years ago when I was there on business." Ben shrugged. "It looked like a lot of fun." He turned to Norma. "And didn't require any more equipment than a broom, which most kids have access to, and a ball."

"Which most kids also have access to." Norma frowned. "Huh. You might be onto something."

"Well, it certainly wouldn't do for me to go throwing money around." Ben grimaced. "That would just end up offending everyone."

"But this way, everyone can participate, without your obvious input."

"Right!"

"I think it's a grand idea, honey. But I want to caution you."

"What?" Ben picked up his spoon.

"I don't want you to overdo things."

"Norma!"

"Seriously, Ben. You know that every time you overextend yourself, you pay for it."

Ben looked at his wife.

"Either you catch a cold, or your legs . . ."

"What's left of them," Ben inserted.

"What's left of them . . ." Norma wrinkled her nose at him, ". . . start to ache and the edges that haven't yet healed get all angry and infected."

Ben made a face.

"I mean it, Ben. I'm happy to see you keeping active, especially under the circumstances. But I don't want you making yourself sick."

Ben sighed and looked at his wife. "Okay, hon. You have my word."

Norma smiled. "I just want you to stay with me for a while."

"And I want to stay with you, sweetheart."

"Good. Then we're on the same page."

"Always and forever." Ben blew her a kiss.

Chapter Five

Ben looked at the two boys watching him intently. "So what do you think?"

"I love it!" Teddy shouted. "Broomball! It'll be so fun!"

"Okay, that's one." Ben smiled as he clapped a hand over an abused ear.

Daniel grinned. "Sounds like a lot of fun, Mr. Frosst. So everyone would be able to play?"

"Everyone that can find – or make – a broom. Do you think the other kids will like the idea?"

"We'll get them all together and then we can ask them!" Daniel headed toward the front door with Teddy hard on his heels.

"Tell them to meet us at the big field!" Ben called.

Daniel waved.

"And I'll go and find your coat." Norma got to her feet.

"Thank you, hon."

Norma hurried from the room and Ben pushed his chair over to the window and rested his forehead against the chill glass. The air outside was still and cold and the branches of the trees were thickly frosted and almost hidden beneath their load of snow. As he watched, a squirrel poked its small head out of a space underneath the lowest branches of a nearby tree and sniffed the air. Then, bushy tail held aloft, it darted across the clearing toward the house, disappearing from Ben's sight.

He sighed. It truly was a beautiful world.

"Here you go, dear." Norma was back.

Ben straightened and smiled at her. "Norma. My ever watchful and helpful sweetheart."

Norma smiled and held out his coat.

He grasped her hand. "I love you," he said softly.

Her smile widened. "And I love you, Ben."

"Forever?"

"Forever."

Ben sighed and, letting go of her hand, slid his arms into his coat. He looked at her as he fastened his buttons. "Are you ready for this?"

"Oh, yes!" Her eyes sparkled. "Lead on!"

* * *

Daniel and Teddy had gathered a large group of children next to the main open field just outside of town. The boys and girls were

[53]

fidgeting and moving around, rubbing mittened hands together and wrapping their arms tightly around themselves to stay warm in the cold, clear air, but all kept their excited eyes on Ben.

"So, you see, it's played much like the game of hockey," Ben was saying. He held out a broom. "But with brooms and boots instead of skates and hockey sticks."

"I'm ready, Mr. Frosst," a young voice piped up from the back. "Let's play!"

Everyone laughed.

"I think we have enough to form six teams," Ben said. "I want each two teams to take a portion of this field and set up two goals."

"But who goes on which team?" someone asked.

"That's for you to sort out," Ben said, grinning. "All I ask is that you try to keep the teams fairly even. Some big players and some small players on each team."

"So no putting all of the big guys onto one team?" Daniel asked.

"Exactly."

In a remarkably short time, three separate games of Broomball were being played across the wide field.

Norma pulled Ben from game to game so he could watch and give advice.

The players quickly learned that brooms with longer bristles were less effective. Several players moved to the side of the field and, using someone's jackknife, shortened the straws by several inches.

"I sure hope they don't get into trouble with their Mamas when they get home," Norma whispered into Ben's ear.

He laughed. "*That* I can help with."

Two of the teams were quite evenly matched and the action was quickly becoming both fast and lethal.

Ben's eyes were shining. "Wow! Those guys have really caught on!"

"Is that what you call it?" Norma winced as two boys collided.

He laughed. "All part of the experience!"

Two younger boys came running up. "Mr. Frosty!" one of them said. "I mean, Mr. Frosst!"

Ben grinned. "Mr. Frosty sounds just fine to me, Leo. What do you need?"

"Mr. Frosst-y, could you come and help us, please. We need a new goalie. Michael's sister just took him home to do chores."

[55]

"Heaven forbid that we stand in the way of 'chores'." Ben laughed. "Okay. Where are you guys playing?"

"We're the game on the end. Next to the wash."

"If you'll give me a hand, we'll arrive together."

The two boys picked up the rope and quickly pulled Ben to the far end of the field. "We've got a goalie!" Leo shouted as they neared. "Mr. Frosty is going to play goal!"

Several of the kids laughed. Then a cheer went up. "Mr. Frosty!"

The two boys pulled Ben to a spot midway between a large, snow-covered bush and a small, struggling tree. Ben looked at the tree. "I apologize in advance for anything I might do to you, little fella."

Leo handed him a broomstick and then ran out onto the field. "We're ready!" he shouted.

The action, which had obviously been suspended when the mysterious 'Michael' had been towed home, commenced. Within seconds, the ball was flying through the air toward Ben.

"Whoa!" he laughed, batting it away with a swing of his broomstick. "These guys are serious!" For the next hour, Ben defended his team's goal against all comers.

A shut-out.

When the shadows began to lengthen, he finally threw his broomstick down. "I think that's enough for today."

The two teams cheered and shook hands with their opposing players.

Ben noticed that the teams playing next to them were also wrapping up their game. The two teams on the far side were still intent, however.

Norma came over and reached for the rope on his sleigh.

Ben chuckled. "They'll probably keep going until it's too dark to see." He nodded toward the last two teams.

Norma followed his gaze. "I expect you're right." Then, noticing several adults walking toward the furiously competing children, she added, "Or until chore time."

Ben laughed.

"I think we'd better get you home, Ben."

"Yeah. I'm getting kind of tired."

Daniel appeared. "I can get you home, Mr. Frosst."

"His name's 'Frosty'!" someone sang out.

Daniel grinned. "Mr. Frosty. I like it."

[57]

Ben laughed. "So do I."

* * *

Through the short winter days, enthusiasm for Broomball continued unabated.

Finally, bowing to pressure, Ben agreed to formalize things a bit. He organized teams according to age and size and made up a schedule. Then, as the need arose, sighed and started a list of rules and regulations.

From morning till night, outside of school hours, the fields in and around town were buzzing with enthusiastic Broomball players.

Ben continued to play goal for many of the teams, happily waving his broomstick for whoever might need him.

Norma smiled at him. "You've become quite the celebrity, Frosty!"

"Speak nicely, woman." Ben grinned. "You're addressing royalty!"

"Yes. From out of the snow, the Snow Man cometh!"

Ben laughed.

"Mr. Frosst. I mean, Mr. Frosty!" Teddy Bering was standing beside his sleigh. Or rather the excited boy was jumping up and down beside Ben's sleigh.

"What is it, Teddy?"

"There's a poster on the billboard, Mr. Frosty! There's going to be a Broomball tournament!"

"Really?" Ben winked at Norma. "Where?"

"Here!" Teddy turned in a little circle, indicating with both arms. "Right in our village!"

"Well this is interesting!"

"Mr. Frosty, can you play on our team?" another small lad had appeared beside Teddy. "That way we can win."

"Well, that all depends on the rules."

"We'll find out!' the two boys charged off.

"Do you think you could? Or should?" Norma's soft voice spoke from behind him.

He turned to look at his wife. "Why not, dear?"

Norma shrugged. "From my understanding of tournaments, they can get quite . . . competitive."

"Well, if you're concerned, then I certainly won't participate. But I did organize it with the understanding that it would be a fun tournament."

Norma smiled. "Good."

"Here it is, Mr. Frosty!" Teddy and his friend had reappeared. Teddy thrust a large, stiff piece of paper under Ben's nose.

"Let me have a look." Ben glanced at the poster. "Well, it says here that it is a Dads' and Kids' tournament. I guess that means I can play!"

"Oh." Teddy's face fell. "We don't have a father. I guess Daniel and I can't play, then."

Ben smiled at the disappointed boy. "Nonsense. You don't have to have a father to be able to play. It just means that fathers *can* play."

Teddy's face lit up. "Really?"

"But I'd be glad to act as your father anyway, so it still wouldn't matter."

"Gee! Wait till I tell Daniel!" Teddy charged off.

"Now look at what you've started," Norma whispered. "This village will never be the same!"

"That is my fondest hope." Ben grinned at her.

* * *

Several teams were formed and practice began in earnest.

Soon, it was difficult to find an open field anywhere in or even near the village that didn't sport a group of men and children intent on honing their skills.

Norma and Ben paused on the street and watched several kids and dads in the central square, broomsticks in their hands, intent on their game.

Norma punched him playfully in the shoulder. "See what you've done?"

Ben rubbed his shoulder and looked at her innocently. "Me?"

"This upcoming tournament has everyone in such a tizzy."

Ben grinned. "Now what's wrong with that?"

Norma snorted softly and pushed Ben's chair up the sidewalk to the grocery store.

A short time later, Ben abandoned his wife in front of the butcher's counter and rolled his chair past the check-out clerk and over to the windows. Outside, brilliant sunshine was glinting off the snow, making it hard to see. Ben shaded his eyes and peered through the glass.

The Broomball players had disappeared on a break and two little girls had taken advantage of their absence and were in the square, creating something out of the only un-trampled patch of fresh snow in sight, their faces were intent as they patted and shaped with mittened hands. Finally one of them stood up, surveying their work with her head tilted to one side. She nodded at her companion and the other girl joined her. Together, they studied their handiwork and broad grins attested to their satisfaction.

Just then, three older boys came down the sidewalk.

Ben recognized Daniel and two of his friends, Neil and Sam.

They stopped beside the two girls and turned to see what was causing all of the excitement.

Laughing, Daniel walked forward and hovered a large foot over whatever the girls had been working on, then slowly leaned forward, obviously threatening their work of art.

Hearing the little girls' raised voices through the thick glass, Ben spun his chair around and headed for the door. Just as Ben reached the sidewalk, Daniel began to wave his arms, as though to regain his balance. "Oh! Oh!" he was saying.

"Don't do it, Dan!" one of the girls screamed. "Don't!"

"But I'm losing my balance!" Dan waved his arms more. "I'm going to fall!"

"Hey!" Ben shouted. "What's going on?"

Everyone on the street, including the three boys, turned to look at him. "Nooooo!" Daniel waved his arms wildly, but lost his balance and fell forward onto his knees. Whatever he had been threatening earlier became a shapeless mass of snow. "Ooops."

One of the girls immediately began to cry. The other, the one who had been screaming at Daniel, walked forward and rammed a booted toe into the fallen boy's backside.

"There, that's what you get, Dan," she said stoutly. "For ruining Joanne's and my sculpture."

Ben stopped his chair on the sidewalk and looked over at the thoroughly embarrassed boy. He raised an eyebrow. "Getting into mischief, Dan?" He shook his head. "That's not like you."

Dan struggled to his feet, his face reddening. "No, Mr. Frosty, I . . . I . . ." His face got redder.

[63]

"You were teasing these little girls and it backfired," Ben said quietly.

"I . . . well . . . yes."

"So you'd better fix it."

Daniel looked over at the mush of snow that used to be a prized work of art. "How?"

Ben smiled. "Recreate it!"

Daniel leaned forward. "I don't know what it was!" he whispered.

Ben laughed. "The girls will help you."

Obediently, Daniel knelt down in the snow and faced the girls. "Can I help you fix it?" he asked. Tears were forgotten and both girls eagerly accepted.

The other two boys joined in and Ben wheeled away. Just as he reached the doors to the grocery, Norma came through them, trailed by a young man holding two paper sacks.

"Oh, there you are, Ben! When I couldn't see you in the store, I assumed you'd be outside."

"You know me well." Ben grinned. He glanced over his shoulder.

[64]

Her eyes followed his. "Anything happening out here?"

The three older boys were meekly carrying out the orders of the two happily-smiling little would-be artists.

"No. Nothing in particular. Just needed to feel the sun on my face."

"Your face is rather pale," Norma frowned at him, then leaned forward and placed her soft cheek against his. "Are you feeling all right?"

"Oh, a little tired. But that's to be expected, isn't it?"

Norma frowned slightly. "I guess so." She sounded doubtful.

* * *

That evening, Norma paused in the doorway to the living room, a book in one hand. "Where are you going?"

Ben smiled at her. "I thought I'd go to bed early. Feeling a bit tired."

Norma walked over and put a slender hand on her husband's forehead. "You're feeling a bit warm, dear. Do you want me to call the doctor?"

Ben shook his head. "No. I'm feeling fine. I just need a good rest."

[65]

Norma stepped back. "Do you want me to come up with you?"

"No, you go ahead and read." Ben waved a hand toward her book.

Norma glanced down and then back at Ben. "All right. But call if you need me."

"I will." Ben pushed the wheels of his chair, moving himself toward the lift on the stairway.

Chapter Six

"That's the second goal! Slowing down today, Ben?"

Ben grinned at the puffing, red-faced man who had stopped beside him. "It can't be me, Fred. I think you guys must be getting faster."

Fred laughed and charged up the field after the rest of men and children.

Ben chuckled and, reaching down, wrapped the blanket a little more securely around him.

He frowned at a red spot on the thick felt.

Blood. He touched it lightly and turned his hand over. It was wet and obviously fresh.

"Something wrong, Ben?"

He looked up. His team coach was standing beside Ben's sleigh. "No. No problem." Ben smiled at him. "But I think I'm done for the day."

The man waved a hand and a young man immediately charged toward them from the sidelines. "Sam will take your place. He's been aching to do it all afternoon!"

Ben laughed. "Then I leave the floor to the bright young man with the big grin," he said, bowing slightly.

"Gee. Thanks, Mr. Frosty!" Sam took Ben's place, immediately assuming an alert posture and staring down the field.

Ben and the coach laughed. "Would you mind giving me a hand?" Ben asked.

His coach immediately grabbed the rope handle and pulled his star player from the field.

"Norma can take me from here."

Norma smiled at the coach. "I can."

The coach grinned and nodded, then went back to the game.

Norma leaned down. "What's the matter?" she asked quietly.

"I seem to be bleeding." Ben said, equally softly. He waved a hand, indicating the telltale patch of red.

Norma glanced down. "Oh, dear. Let's get you home."

* * *

Rob was frowning thoughtfully. "Your one leg has never healed satisfactorily. I'd like to do some blood work and make sure that everything is all right."

[68]

Ben sighed and nodded. "I guess another poke or two in the grand scheme of things isn't going to change my life."

Rob raised his eyebrows. "It might."

Ben shrugged and held out one arm. "Go ahead and bleed me dry, doc."

Rob shook his head and reached for his medical kit. "You know, the skin grafts on your one leg have healed beautifully." He started to lay out what he needed. "I can't figure out why the other one seems to be having such difficulty."

"Ornery?" Norma suggested. "Like its owner?"

Ben laughed. "What is it that they say about the limb and the man being made of similar material…?"

Norma rolled her eyes. "*They* don't say anything about it. You just made that up."

"Well, it's true. Ouch!"

Rob grimaced. "Sorry. There, I'm all done."

Ben rubbed his arm. "Quack! I guess I know now why they always have the nurses do that."

"Sticks and stones . . ." Rob made a face at his friend.

Ben grinned.

Rob packed up his equipment. "I'll let you know when the tests come back."

"Sounds good."

"Oh, by the way, Harriett and I would like to invite the two of you over to dinner on Thursday. Can you make it?"

Norma smiled. "If I can tear him away from whatever Broomball game he might be playing, we'd love to come."

"Good. Harriett said to tell you she's having Gertrude make something yummy."

Ben grinned. "I like yummy."

Rob grinned back. "Well, then this will be a good time to come."

"What time?" Norma asked. "And what can we bring?"

"Nothing. Well, except for His Nibs here."

Norma smiled. "Oh, I probably couldn't get out of the house without him now."

"Yeah. Now that I know what's being served!" Ben laughed.

"I'll see you Thursday, then. About seven?"

"We'll be there," Norma said.

"Hopefully, I'll have your results before then, but if not, I'll have them there."

"Good," Ben said. "See you when we see you!" He closed the door after their friend.

* * *

"Come in! Come in!" Rob swung the door wide.

The twin flavours of beef and roasting onions wafted out to the two on the front step. Ben grinned at Norma. "I think we've found the place, hon!"

"It certainly smells good." Norma handed their host her coat. "Be polite and hand Rob your coat, Ben," she whispered loudly.

"I don't have to be polite to Rob!" Ben whispered back. "He's just my doctor!"

Rob cleared his throat and all three of them laughed.

Soon, they were seated in Rob's and Harriett's comfortable living room as Harriett, small, round and dark-haired with smiling green eyes, bustled in. "How nice of the two of you to come." She gave Norma a hug. "Rob and I have been meaning to invite you for ages." She held out one plump, white hand to Ben. "Welcome!"

Rob moved over to the bar. "Would anyone care for a drink? I'm buying."

"Just ice water for each of us," Norma said. "Doctor's orders."

[71]

Rob looked at his wife. "Did you hear that, sweetheart? People who actually listen to their doctor!"

Harriett laughed. "It's a miracle!"

A short time later, the four of them were seated around the table as Rob's and Harriet's maid brought in the first course.

"Mmmm. Salad! My favourite!" Ben said.

Norma leaned toward him. "You always say that!" she whispered.

"It's always true!"

It was a pleasant evening of friends associating with friends.

But, after the dishes had been cleared, Rob looked at Ben and stood up. "I need to talk to you for a moment, Ben. Professionally."

"Oh-oh." Ben winked at his wife.

Norma frowned slightly and clutched instinctively for Ben's hand.

"Would you rather we take this into my office?"

Ben glanced at Norma, then at Harriett. "Nope. No one but friends and family here." He smiled. "I'd really rather you told me here. I always get things mixed up when I try to re-tell."

Rob smiled slightly and nodded. "You're the boss."

[72]

Ben grinned. "And don't you forget it!"

Rob resumed his chair. "Ben, I don't know why your one leg isn't healing. The blood tests were inconclusive. You have some sort of infection that is preventing you from healing properly."

"But we've been doing everything you told us to do!" Norma protested. "The cleaning, disinfecting and swabbing."

Ben laughed. "Yeah, we've been doing lots of swabbing."

Rob shrugged. "I don't know the whys. I only know what is."

"Well, that's a poor answer. I'll just have to find myself another doctor."

Rob stiffened. "If you wish."

Ben punched him playfully . "Oh come on, Rob! I'm only kidding. You know I trust you completely."

Rob snorted softly. "You're right. I do know. It's just that your case has gotten me so . . . frustrated."

Harriett put a hand on her husband's arm, then looked at Ben. "He really has been working hard to try to help you," she said softly.

Ben was quick to reassure both of his friends. "I know it, Harriett. Rob's a friend first." He pushed his chair back slightly from the table. "So what's the prognosis, Doc? What do you want me to do?"

"Well, I'd like to put you back into the hospital and try another graft."

Ben raised his eyebrows. "Another graft?"

"Well, it wouldn't be as extensive as the initial grafts. We'd only be working with the infected area."

Ben smiled. "Well, that's a relief!"

"We'll cut back the infected tissue and graft in new."

"Ick. Spare me the details, doc. Just tell me what time to be there."

* * *

A week later, Ben twitched the covers of his hospital bed. "So Rob thinks things went very well." He shuffled around uncomfortably, then leaned toward his wife. "My backside hurts."

Norma smiled. "Is that where they took the skin?"

Ben straightened and lifted his head to a lofty angle. "A gentleman never tells."

"This same gentleman who just finished telling me that his backside hurt?"

[74]

Ben laughed. "Erm . . . well . . . yes. That would be the one."

Norma laughed. "I'm so glad he's so fastidious and protective of my girlish sensibilities."

"Yes, aren't I. But back to my original statement, Rob thinks things went well. He says I'll be out of here in plenty of time for the tournament."

"I'm so glad." She sighed. "I'm getting rather weary of bad news."

Ben grinned. "I don't think anyone *likes* bad news, hon."

"Well, you know what I mean."

"I do. But it's all behind us now."

Norma summoned up a smile. "I hope so," she said, softly.

Chapter Seven

Norma glanced out the window as she spooned up hot oatmeal. "Well, it looks as though you've got a beautiful day for the tournament."

Ben nodded. "Couldn't ask for better."

"You're not eating, dear." Norma looked at his untouched breakfast. "Are you all right?"

"I'm fine, hon. Don't fuss." Ben put a hand to his forehead. "I just didn't sleep very well last night."

"Too much on your mind?"

"Probably. This tournament ended up being a lot bigger than I bargained for."

"I heard that you have teams from as far away as Salt Springs."

"There is even a team from Romeo! Broomball has really caught on!"

"It's because it takes so little to participate. You don't have to buy any special equipment."

Ben smiled and nodded. "Most households have at least one broom. And if there is more than one player, a broom is easily constructed after one walk through the woods."

Norma smiled back. "I'm so glad you started all of this. It has made a big difference to so many of the children . . . and parents . . . in this town."

Ben smiled. "And to me, too." He glanced at the clock. "Well, I guess I'd better get going. My team is in the first of the matches."

"Are you sure you're up to this?" Norma asked anxiously, putting a hand on his arm.

Ben looked at her. "I'm sure, hon. Trust me. If I start feeling poorly, I'll quit."

Norma nodded and dropped her hand. "I'll be along later to watch."

* * *

Their assigned field was completely surrounded by a dense gathering of spectators. Ben's team pulled him through the crush and onto the playing area and Ben looked around. "If I'd known it was going to be this crazy, I probably would have thought twice about starting it all."

Daniel, who was pulling on the rope, looked back. "Yeah, Mr. Frosty. You would have thought twice and done it anyway!"

Ben grinned. "You know me well."

[77]

Daniel stopped. "One of the guys was telling me that the other fields are just as crowded as this one."

Ben raised his eyebrows. "Maybe we're onto something, Dan."

Daniel smiled. "I think we are, Mr. Frosty."

The referee, dressed in a red and white striped tunic, walked to the middle of the field and blew on his whistle. "Teams! Take your places!"

Ben rubbed his hands together. "Well, here we go!"

* * *

"Ben, you're soaking wet!" Norma's face was pinched with concern.

"It was a tough game," Ben said mildly, grinning at her. A trickle of blood ran down his cheek.

"And you're hurt!" Norma pulled a handkerchief from her pocket and began to dab at it.

Ben smiled at her. "It's just a scratch. Someone caught me in a back swing just at the end of the game."

"Ben! You could have been hurt!"

"Goes with the territory. Actually, it was just the bristles that caught me. One scratched a little deeper is all."

[78]

Norma peered at his injury. "Oh. You're right. It's already stopped bleeding. Well, let's get you out of those soaking things before you catch a chill."

Ben looked around. "And where do you propose we go to do that?"

People were everywhere. Crowds watching the current game, teams milling about waiting their next turn and small children darting around and through. "The only privacy we can hope to find will be back at the house."

Norma picked up the rope to his sled. "Then that's where we'll go."

"Norma, stop," Ben said, laughing. "Here. Hand me my clean sweater."

Norma laid the heavy sweater onto his outstretched hands. "You're not going to . . ."

But Ben had already stripped off his wet jersey. "Brrrr!" he said. With swift movements, he donned the dry one. "Ahh. That's more like it!" He pulled his coat on over top. "There. You see? Good as new." He snuggled in his coat. "Blissfully warm!"

Norma smiled at him. "So you won?"

"Barely." Ben handed her a piece of paper. "That team from Salt Springs was tough."

Norma looked at the paper. "So this is how a tournament is organized."

"Well, the good ones." Ben grinned.

"So your team goes here?" She pointed to a blank space in the line-up.

"Yeah. And the Salt Springs team goes there." He pointed.

Norma traced, first one side, then the other, with a slender finger. "Huh. You might have to face them again. Providing you both win all of your matches."

Ben grinned. "Yeah and they will probably be even tougher then". He sighed. "Pay back is so sweet."

Norma shivered.

* * *

"Oh, Ben, they are twice as big as you are!"

Ben's team was once more facing the big Salt Springs players for the championship game.

The decider.

He laughed. "Well, I'm only half as big as I used to be! So that doesn't mean anything."

Norma made a face. "You know what I mean. Look at little Suzi. She barely comes to that boy's waist!"

"Well Suzi certainly won't be facing him. We'll be careful to match her with someone closer to her own size."

"Huh. The only person close to her own size is you, Ben!"

They both laughed.

Just then, the whistle blew.

"Can you get me into position?" Ben asked. Norma grabbed the rope and slid her husband's sled into the goal area. "Good. Thanks, hon." he reached out a hand and pulled her toward him.

She leaned over and kissed him. "You be careful, Ben."

"Always."

Norma joined the spectators on the sidelines as the referee dropped the hard, red ball, and the action started.

Ben's little team was hopelessly outmatched, almost from the start. The Salt Springs players controlled the action from the first ball drop to the final whistle. Ben's team managed to keep the visitors to only four goals, but the local team's final defeat was inevitable.

The only bright point for the local fans came when little Suzi sneaked unseen between two of the big Salt Springs players and scored her team's only goal, just moments before the game ended.

Even though they had been soundly defeated, her team carried her triumphantly from the field, cheering wildly.

Norma hurried over to a smiling, but obviously tired Ben. "Are you all right?"

"Sound as a dollar. However sound that is!"

"Here. Let's get you changed again!" Norma pulled yet another warm, dry sweater out of her large bag and quickly helped Ben into it. "There. Warm and dry."

"Thanks, hon." He reached out a hand and grasped her mittened fingers. "You're an angel!"

"And don't you forget it." Norma grinned at him.

"Ben? We're ready to start the awards ceremony."

Both Ben and Norma turned. "Ah, Mayor!" Ben held out his hand. "So glad you could be here for this!"

"Wouldn't have missed it!" He shook Ben's hand. "I just wish I could have been here for the whole thing." He smiled down at Ben. "But at least I got to see the last game!"

Ben made a face. "Yes. Well. I wish you could have seen some real playing."

The Mayor raised his eyebrows. "Real playing? Oh, believe me, I did. When little Suzi Brinks stole that ball from those two big players, I almost had a heart attack!"

Ben grinned. "As did we all, Mayor."

"That made the game for everyone," the Mayor went on. "Who won or lost didn't matter at all at that point."

Ben nodded.

"People!" someone shouted. "People, we want to start the awards ceremony!"

Ben looked up. Someone was standing on one of the picnic tables at the far end of the field, waving his arms. Everyone had started to move toward him.

"I'd better get over there," the Mayor whispered. "Can I pull you along, Ben?"

[83]

Ben glanced at Norma, who nodded, smiled and handed the rope to the Mayor. "Be our guest."

The Mayor pulled Ben's sleigh to the edge of the gathering crowd and stopped it beside the tables, then joined two other people now standing on top of the nearest one and shouted for quiet.

The crowd complied slowly.

"Well, I'd say this has been a good day," he said.

Cheers broke out.

He raised his hands and they quieted. "I want to thank all of you for your participation today. And for the great sportsmanship and fine playing we saw."

Another cheer.

"Would the winning team please come forward?" The Salt Springs players immediately crowded around his table, grinning, shaking hands and slapping backs.

The Mayor invited their team captain up onto the table beside him and the two shook hands. Then the Mayor looked down into the rest of the smiling faces gathered closely around. "You fathers and daughters and sons all played hard today," he said. "Played well. And it is my privilege to present you with this trophy."

A man on the other side of him, lifted something out of a box. A gleaming, golden cup, with a carved, wooden base.

The Mayor held it up. "Your team's name will go here." He pointed. "And as you can see, there is space for many, many more names." He looked around. "Because we're going to make this an annual tournament!"

The cheering was louder this time. People jumping up and down and waving their hands in the air.

The Mayor finally clapped his hands and order was once more restored. "So, team, this year, it's yours." He again shook hands with the captain, then, finally, handed him the large trophy and grinned. "But next year, watch out! The challenge is on!"

More cheering.

The Salt Springs team captain held the cup aloft and his team shouted loudly as the crowd parted for them to make their triumphant parade around the field. But instead, the Salt Springs captain waved for quiet.

The crowd subsided, watching him.

"There is one person to whom this trophy should be dedicated," he said. "The one person who made this day, this tournament, possible." He looked down at Ben, sitting quietly beside the table. "People, our team dedicates this win to Mr. Frosst. Frosty, our Snowman!"

The crowd went wild as they cheered and laughed and cried.

Daniel and Teddy appeared beside Ben, handed him his broom, slapped his top hat on his head, then grabbed the rope and pulled him out into the field. The Salt Springs team fell in behind them, their captain proudly carrying their trophy.

They did an entire circuit of the field with Ben being pulled proudly by his two greatest fans and the Salt Springs and the rest of the teams stringing out behind them.

Then Daniel nodded at Teddy and the two of them continued out one end of the field and into the village itself. Laughing and cheering, the teams followed them and then the rest of the crowd fell in behind.

An impromptu parade!

The brothers, pulling Ben, marched proudly up one street and down another, with the rest of the people laughing and singing behind them.

Finally, they started up main street.

[86]

At the crossroads, an officer was directing traffic. He turned and stared as they approached, then held up one hand and blew his whistle. "Stop!" he shouted.

Daniel and Teddy paused and Ben leaned out, lifted both hands and grinned at the officer who laughed and, an instant later stepped back and waved them through.

Laughing, the brothers started forward once more, the crowd behind them.

Surprised motorists, waiting for a break in the traffic, stared at the long line of people who saluted and waved as they passed.

Finally, the parade wound its way to Ben and Norma's house. Daniel and Teddy pulled the sleigh to the side of the street and let the crowd go past them, Ben shaking hands with as many as he could and waving happily to the rest.

Finally, the last of the crowd passed by and disappeared up the street.

Norma watched them go. "Well, I guess that's that."

"I guess it is," Ben agreed. He sighed. "What a wonderful day!"

Daniel started forward. "I think we should probably get you back inside."

[87]

Ben made a face. "I guess we should. It's a shame to end such a nice day, but I guess all good things must have a finish."

"But think of what you've started," Daniel said. "Now, every year, when we have our Broomball tournament, everyone will think of you."

Ben grinned. "But more importantly, they will be playing Broomball. Come on, let's get inside. I'm hungry!"

* * *

That evening, Ben and Norma were relaxing beside a glowing fire, hot chocolate in hand, talking about the day.

"When little Suzi stole that ball right out from under those two big players, I almost died," Ben said.

Norma laughed. "As did everyone in the crowd."

"It sure put the capper on the day."

"Mr. Ben?"

Both of them turned to see Missy in the doorway. "There's a phone call for you, sir," she said. "Someone calling from the hospital."

"The hospital!" Ben wheeled himself quickly out of the room, across the front hall and into his office. He grabbed the telephone receiver lying on the broad desk.

"Hello?" he barked into the phone.

Someone spoke for a few moments.

"When did this happen?" Ben's hand tightened around the receiver.

Norma stared at her husband's white face. "What?" she mouthed.

Ben shook his head briefly. "Don't they have anyone else?"

There was a pause while the person responded.

Then, "Never mind. Norma and I will be right over."

He banged down the phone. "Missy!" he bellowed.

Norma jumped. "Ben, what is it?"

Missy appeared in the doorway, rather breathless. "What's the matter, Mr. Ben?"

"Get our coats. Quickly!" Ben wheeled himself back into the hall.

"Ben, what is it?" Norma followed quickly.

Ben looked at Norma and she was surprised to see tears pooling in his dark eyes. "Daniel and Teddy are at the hospital and asking for me. It's about their mom. The doctors think she's had a heart

attack."

Chapter Eight

"Ben!" Norma was horrified. "But is she . . . will she be . . .?"
She left the question dangling as Missy bustled in with their coats.

There was a pinched frown between Ben's eyebrows. "We'll talk
in the car. Thank you Missy. Sorry for the hurry."

"That's all right, Mr. Ben. You'll tell me about it later."

Ben smiled briefly. "I will, Missy." He pulled on his coat as
Norma donned hers. "We'd better hurry."

Norma nodded and pushed him out the front door.

* * *

"Oh, Mr. Frosty!" Teddy jumped up from his chair and rushed
across the waiting room.

Ben caught a brief glimpse of a tear-streaked face before the boy
threw his arms around Ben's chest. He tightened his arms about the
boy and pulled him into his lap. "I'm here, Teddy. I'm here."

For several minutes, the boy sobbed against him.

Ben reached up with one hand and stroked the light head. "It'll
be all right, Teddy," he whispered.

Daniel came into the waiting room, carrying a steaming cup.
"Oh, Mr. Frosty!" He quickly set the cup down, sloshing some of its

contents onto a low table. Then he pulled a chair over beside Ben and sat as closely as he could.

Ben reached out a hand and grasped Daniel's. "How is she?" He felt Teddy's arms tighten.

Daniel shook his head. "I don't know, Mr. Frosty. They haven't told me anything." Tears made streaks down the smooth cheeks as he slumped down in his chair.

"Well, I'm sure everything will be all right," Ben tried to sound reassuring. "These sorts of things always look far worse than they are."

Daniel looked over at the wall. "She was just lying there. By the woodpile."

"Woodpile?" Norma asked.

"Yeah. Teddy and I couldn't find her when we first got home. We figured that she must have had to work late."

He brushed at his face with one hand. "She was so mad that she had to work today when she wanted to watch us play in the tournament." Norma gave him a handkerchief and he scrubbed at his face and blew his nose. "Then Teddy noticed that there were a couple of kettles on the stove and that other preparations for supper had been started. We realized that she must have come home. That's when we started to look for her."

Ben smoothed Teddy's hair. "And she had gone out to the woodpile?"

"Yeah, that's where we found her," Daniel said. "Lying in the snow."

Norma frowned. "Well, if the kettles were still boiling on the stove, she couldn't have been out there long."

"That's what the doctor said." Daniel shook his head. "But she was awfully cold."

Ben and Norma were silent for a moment.

Teddy suddenly lifted his head. "Mr. Frosty?"

Ben looked down at him. "What is it, Teddy?"

"Who will look after us now?"

Ben glanced at Norma, then looked at Teddy. "Don't you have any other family, Teddy?"

Teddy shook his head. "We don't have anyone but Mom. We used to have Grampa. But he died."

"Well, don't you worry about that at all." Ben tightened his arms around the boy. "Someone will be there to look after you and your brother."

Teddy relaxed against Ben.

For several minutes, they sat there, silently praying for the woman fighting for her life in the next room.

Then a door in the far wall opened and a man dressed in surgical scrubs came into the nearly-empty room and glanced around. Seeing that they were the only people in the room, he came toward them.

Ben summoned up a smile. "Hello, Byron. Any news?"

Byron nodded, then turned to Daniel and Teddy. "Are you the family of Grace Bering?" he asked the older boy.

Daniel got to his feet and nodded. "She's our mom, sir."

The doctor sighed. "I'm so very sorry. But your mom didn't . . ." He rubbed a hand across his eyes. "She's dead, son."

Daniel stared at the doctor for a moment. Then he sank back into his chair and, pulling his legs up, curled himself into a tight, little ball.

Teddy began to cry again.

[94]

The doctor looked at Ben and Norma. "Are you and Norma family members as well, Ben?"

Ben looked at Norma. Then, "Yes. We are."

"Well, I will have to speak to you about . . . things." The doctor glanced at the two boys. "But for now, are you taking responsibility for these two boys?"

Norma nodded. "We are."

"Well, I suggest that you get them home and into bed. They've had a terrible shock."

"Yes." Ben tightened his hold on the sobbing boy in his arms. "If you can help Daniel, hon. I've got Teddy."

* * *

Two days later, Ben leaned back in his wheelchair and looked at Rob, seated comfortably on the couch in the living room. "So what will happen to them?"

Rob shrugged. "In the absence of other family members, they will have to go to an orphanage."

Norma dabbed at her eyes with a fine handkerchief. "So young to have lost everyone. First their dad, a couple of years ago in that accident."

[95]

Rob nodded. "And now this." He shook his head. "I would say that the orphanage is their only option."

Ben cleared his throat. "I would agree with you. And that is why Norma and I want to take the boys."

Rob smiled. "I thought you would say something like that." He pursed his lips and frowned thoughtfully. "I don't think the courts will have any problem granting your petition provided you can make a good case."

Ben glanced at Norma's anxious face and grinned. "Oh, I think we can make a good case."

Rob got to his feet. "Well, I'm happy to get things rolling. I'll make some calls and I'm sure someone will be in touch."

* * *

That evening, Teddy looked up from his uneaten dinner. "So we can stay with you?"

Norma touched the boy's shoulder gently. "If that's what you want, dear."

Teddy looked across at Daniel, who smiled and nodded.

Teddy looked back at Norma. "Are you kidding? That's what Dan 'n me have been praying for!"

Norma smiled and smoothed his hair with a trembling hand. "Have you, dear? It's what Ben and I have been praying for, too."

Ben looked at the boys. "I hope you understand what we are telling you. We don't just want you to stay here. We want to adopt you as well."

"Adopt?" Teddy wrinkled his brow. "What's that mean?"

Norma leaned toward him. "It means you would belong to us. You would really be our boys."

Ben nodded. "You would . . . well . . . you *could*, even change your last name to Frosst."

Teddy stared at him. "We'd be Daniel Frosst and Teddy Frosst?"

Norma glanced at Daniel, then back to Teddy. "Only if you want it, dear. You can keep Bering if you'd rather."

Again, Teddy looked at his brother.

"Do you think Mom would be mad at us if we used your name?" Daniel asked.

Ben smiled. "Absolutely not. You'd still belong to your family! It's just that it would make things easier for you now. At school. And at . . ."

"Doctor's appointments," Norma put in.

[97]

"Yeah." Ben grinned. "And for anything . . . legal."

The boys looked at each other. Daniel frowned. "Can we think about this?"

Norma smiled. "Of course, dear. For as long as you want."

"But what do you think about the adoption?" Ben asked.

Teddy frowned. "You're sure Mom wouldn't be mad at us for being your boys?"

Norma smiled at the earnest face. "She'd just be happy to know that her two beautiful boys were being looked after . . ."her voice caught, ". . . and loved," she finished finally.

Daniel nodded.

Teddy looked at Norma. "Okay." He got to his feet and held out his hand.

Norma gripped it.

He shook her hand solemnly. "There. A gen . . . gennel . . . gentleman's agreement."

Daniel came over and did the same. Then both boys walked around the table to Ben and repeated the gesture.

"So is it done now?" Teddy asked Ben.

[98]

Ben smiled. "Well, there are a few things to do yet. We have to fill out the paperwork and then go and see the judge."

Teddy's eyes got big. "A judge? Like a real judge. Who does murders and stuff?"

Ben grinned. "Don't worry, Teddy, they don't usually eat small boys."

"Well, not without sauce anyway." Norma smiled.

* * *

Light seeped in through the partially-closed slotted blinds, relieving the dimness only slightly. Ben looked around the room, furnished with dusty, heavy oak furniture and massive floor-to-ceiling bookshelves. He sighed. "The law is supposed to be complicated and cumbersome."

Norma made a face. "Yeah, but not right now!" She squirmed uncomfortably on the hard, wooden bench and dabbed at her cheeks with a spotless handkerchief.

Ben put out his hand and patted his wife's arm. "It'll work out, hon. I promise you."

She smiled at him tentatively. "What do you suppose the Judge is saying to those two?"

[99]

Ben shrugged. "Talking to them about their feelings."

"But why send us out?"

He sighed. "I suppose he wants them uninfluenced."

Norma snorted and slid to her feet. "As if we would influence them negatively!" She began to pace restlessly.

"Well, he doesn't know that."

Norma stopped, put both hands on her hips, and looked at him. "Ben, Tom has known you since you took your first step - pardon the example - and he knows that we aren't a pair of criminals bent on ruining those boys!"

Ben grinned at his wife. "I love it when you get indignant. Your face turns a lively pink and your eyes flash." He tipped his head to one side. "It's quite intoxicating."

"Ben, focus!"

He laughed. "I am, hon, I am," he said, soothingly. He waved a hand. "I'm sure all of this is mere formality."

Norma plunked herself back down on the hard, uninviting bench. "Formality!" she scoffed.

Ben rolled his chair closer. "I know how much this means to you, Norma."

"Oh, Ben, it means everything to me! My one chance to be a mother!"

Ben was silent and Norma gasped and reached for his hands. "I'm sorry, my darling! I am! I . . . I . . . wasn't thinking."

"I know how hard my accident has been for you, hon. You have been a pillar of strength. Despite the tearing disappointment you have been suffering." He leaned closer and squeezed her hands. "It'll all come right."

She dabbed at her eyes and looked at him. "Oh, Ben, I do love you!"

"And I love you," Ben said tenderly.

Just then, the doors behind them opened and a tall, grey-haired, stoop-shouldered man in a rather crumpled suit appeared. He glanced into the hallway and waved to Ben and Norma.

"Could you and your good wife please step back into my office, Ben?"

Tears forgotten, Norma sprang to her feet and quickly pushed Ben's chair through the doorway.

Daniel and Teddy were standing to one side of the large, heavily-carved desk which dominated the room.

[101]

Both of them were smiling broadly.

The Judge walked around behind his desk, but didn't sit down. For a few seconds, he shuffled some papers. Then he straightened and levelled a look at, first Ben, then Norma, then the two boys. "I'm ready to pronounce sentence," he said soberly.

Teddy gasped.

A small smile briefly kinked one corner of the stern face, and was as quickly gone. "I'm going to sentence the four of you to days of hardship, sickness, disappointment, sleeplessness, pain and anguish."

Teddy's face was a study in dismay.

The Judge went on, "But along with that, I'm also sentencing you to contentment, laughter, happiness, health, hard work, victories, triumphs and joy indescribable. Oh, and lots and lots of love." He smiled. "Believe me, the joys will infinitely outweigh the sorrows."

Teddy was smiling once more.

The Judge moved out from behind his desk and joined the two boys, placing a hand on each shoulder. "We had a very nice chat and these two boys have informed me that they are very willing to become part of your family, Ben. You and your wife have my deepest and most heartfelt congratulations!"

Norma burst into tears.

Ben grinned widely. "Well . . . that . . ." he cleared his throat and tried again. "That is good news," he managed finally.

The boys ran across the room and the four of them shared their first hug as a family.

"Is it all right to call you Dad, now?" Teddy asked.

"Shoo!" the judge said, grinning. "Get out of my office and start being happy!"

Chapter Nine

The small boy's face was a study. "Who's the guy in the sleigh?"

"That's my dad!" Teddy said proudly.

"What happened to his legs?"

"Oh, he was in a bad bus accident and they got crushed." Daniel

had joined them. "They had to get cut off just above his knees."

"Oh." The boy looked at Daniel. "Is he your dad, too?"

"Yup. Want to meet him?"

"Well, I'm not sure . . ."

"C'mon." Teddy took the boy's hand. "His name is Frosty!"

"Frosty? I've heard of him! He's the guy who . . ."

"Started all of this. Yeah." Daniel laughed. "Come on. Quick.

Before the practice starts."

"Dad! Dad! This guy wants to meet you!" Teddy towed the

smaller boy toward Ben.

Ben looked up. "Sorry, coach," he said to the man beside him.

"I'll just have a quick word with my boys."

The coach grinned and walked away.

"Well, hello, young man. What's your name?"

Teddy spoke up. "His name is Wendell. His family just moved here."

"My dad got a job," Wendell said, shyly.

Ben smiled. "Well, that is good to hear. So, Wendell, do you want to play Broomball?"

Wendell turned to look at the kids warming up on the field behind them. "I don't know. I've never played before."

"Don't worry about it," Teddy told him. "Neither had we until a couple of months ago!" He waved one arm, indicating the broad field behind them, busy with intent players. "Now look at us!"

Just then, one of the players on the field tripped and ploughed into another and both went down in a giggling heap.

Wendell blinked. "Oh!"

Ben laughed. "Maybe you should look some other time. Here, son, take my broomstick. Teddy and Daniel will explain things to you."

Teddy looked at Ben. "But aren't you going to need your stick, Dad?"

"Not right now, son. I'm going to watch for a while."

[105]

"Okay." Teddy looked doubtful. He turned slowly toward the field. "C'mon, Wendell."

A while later, Norma arrived to find a shivering Ben. "Cold, dear?"

"Freezing. I didn't realize how cold it is out here when one isn't working up a sweat!"

"Well, let's get you home!" She looked up. "Dan, honey! Teddy!"

The two boys left their game and ran over.

"I'm taking Dad home."

Daniel reached for Teddy's broom. "Do you want us to come now?"

"No. You finish your practice. I'll get Dad home and get him warmed up."

"Okay!" the two boys charged off.

"But come home for supper as soon as you're finished!"

Daniel waved a hand.

"Let's get you home." She picked up the rope and began pulling the sleigh. A short time later, they were sitting in their living room, beside a crackling fire.

Norma smoothed Ben's hair. "Better?"

"Much!" Ben grinned. He stretched his hands out to the flames. "I think I'm starting to thaw out."

Missy bustled in carrying a tray. "Right here, Missy."

The woman set the tray on the closest table.

"Thank you, Missy."

"Yes. Thank you," Ben said, fervently. "This will finish the job!"

Missy smiled and disappeared.

"Here, dear. Nice and hot." Norma handed Ben a cup of hot chocolate. "Guaranteed to cure what ails you."

"Huh. So *this* is the magic elixir. Just imagine! And we've had it all along."

Norma laughed.

Ben shivered suddenly and set his cup down.

"Ben? Are you all right?"

He bundled himself deeper into the warm blanket his wife had draped around his shoulders. "I'm fine, hon. Just having a bit of a time getting warm."

"Well, drink your hot chocolate. It's not doing you any good sitting there."

A short time later, Ben threw off his blanket.

"Finally warmed up, have you?"

"Really warm."

Norma turned from her study of the flames and looked at her husband. "Ben, your face is all flushed!"

"It's really warm. *I'm* really warm."

"I'm calling Rob." Norma set her cup on the table and picked up the phone.

* * *

Rob frowned at his friend, as he dropped a thermometer into a little container and capped it tightly. "And you've been feeling all right till now?"

"I have Rob. Just fine."

Norma looked at her husband for a moment, then turned to Rob. "Well, he has been a bit tired."

"Well, that's just because of the tournament, and . . ." Ben glanced across the bedroom at the two boys standing just inside the door, ". . . other things."

Rob grinned at him. "Well, you certainly manage to accomplish more than any two other men in this village. But you shouldn't be overdoing it."

"I'm not overdoing it!" Ben said in his best indignant voice.

"Dad? Are you all right?" Teddy's small voice cracked slightly. The boy was obviously worried.

"I'm fine, son. Come over here, you two, and stop hovering in the doorway!"

The boys approached the bed hesitantly.

"Come on, guys. It's me! You don't have to be scared!"

Teddy darted ahead of Daniel and plunked himself down on the foot of the bed. Daniel joined him a bit more slowly, finally stopping just beside his brother.

Ben sighed. "I'm just running a temperature. It happens to everyone." He glanced around and laughed. "I don't know when I've ever seen such a bunch of gloomy faces."

Norma hitched closer. "Well, we're worried about you, dear."

Teddy nodded. "Yeah, Dad. I don't want you to get sick."

Ben rolled his eyes. "I'm not getting sick! I'll be up and about before you can say 'Jack Robinson'.

[109]

"Why would I want to say that?" Teddy looked confused.

"It's a figure of speech, dear," Norma said, smiling. "It just means that he'll get better really soon."

"Oh. Okay." Teddy screwed up his face and closed his eyes. "Jack Robinson." He curled both hand into fists and pumping them up and down with each chant. "Jack Robinson. Jack Robinson."

Ben and Norma laughed. Ben looked at his wife. "What did we ever do for entertainment before these two showed up?" He reached for Teddy and Daniel's hands. "Don't worry boys. I'll be better in the morning."

*　*　*

A few days later, Norma sat down across from Rob in her front room and sighed. "It's a nightmare, Rob. His graft, the new one, is all red and infected. Can't you figure out what's doing this?"

Rob shook his head. "I think it's the same infection we've been fighting all along. Only now, it's turned septic."

"What does that mean?"

"It's entered his bloodstream. Sepsis is poisoning of the blood."

"Poisoning?" Norma went pale. "What can we do?"

[110]

"Well, he's refusing to go to the hospital. So I'm going to start him on a course of the new antibiotics here. But I don't have to tell you that I'm getting quite worried."

* * *

"Ben?"

Ben opened his eyes. "Sorry. Did I doze off?" he mumbled.

Norma smiled slightly. "A couple of hours ago, dear."

"Sorry."

"It's fine, dear. But Teddy is here. He wants to read you a story he wrote."

A smile broke across Ben's pale face. "Story? Good."

"Come, Teddy. Daddy's ready."

Teddy appeared beside her. He climbed up onto the bed and snuggled down on the pillows beside Ben.

Norma smoothed Teddy's dark hair, nodded at the two of them and left the room.

"I wrote this, Dad."

Ben smiled. "Good."

"It's called 'Family'."

Ben smiled again. "Good title."

[111]

Teddy giggled. "You want me to just read it, or do you want to see the pictures"

"Definitely want pictures."

"Okay!" Teddy shuffled some papers.

"See, Dad? This is the cover. It's you-" (he pointed to a figure in a wheelchair) "-and Norma-mom and Daniel and me."

Ben nodded. "Nice. Good work."

Teddy beamed and turned the page. "Once upon a time, there were two boys."

He showed another picture, this one featuring three figures. "These two boys had a mom."

He flipped the page. "They really wanted a dad." He showed a picture of a shadowy, indistinct figure. "Someone to play sports with them and to do Dad stuff."

"There was a man in town who did things with them." Teddy turned over another paper. This picture featured a man in a sleigh.

Ben smiled. "Looks like me."

"It is you, Dad!" He turned back to his papers. "This man loved the two boys and helped them."

Ben reached out a hand and clasped the small, dimpled one so close by. "He did love them."

Teddy turned another page. "And the two boys were happy."

He held up a picture of two figures, each wearing broad smiles.

"But then their Mom got sick and died." Teddy showed a picture of a small, huddled figure, lying in the snow. "And went to live with the angels."

Ben blinked his eyes rapidly, then dabbed at them with the sheet.

"The two boys were very sad." Another picture of two figures, with little, blue droplets falling from their eyes.

"But the man came and told them that they could be his boys." Two figures, again with broad smiles.

"And the boys were happy." Another picture of four figures. One in a wheelchair.

"There, Dad! What do you think?"

"Perfect, son. Perfect. So proud of you!"

Teddy beamed and shuffled his papers again. "You really liked it?"

"Really did."

"What was your favourite part?"

"When the boys were happy."

Teddy grinned at him. "That's my favourite part, too." He snuggled close to Ben.

"Teddy, do you like it here?" Ben asked suddenly.

"I love it here, Dad!" Teddy sounded excited. "I have my own room and my own bed and my own toys."

"Do you . . . do you . . . miss your mom?"

Teddy frowned thoughtfully. "Sometimes. She would always read to me and make me good stuff to eat." He looked at Ben. "Norma-mom does the same things. Except that Missy makes the yummy things."

"Do you love Norma-mom?"

"I do, Dad. And so does Daniel. He loves to talk to her. Our Mom never had much time to talk. She always had to work."

"You had no one else. She . . . had to do it."

"I know." Teddy looked sad. "But sometimes, I wished that she could be home more. Like Norma-mom is."

Ben smiled. Then he took a deep breath. "Teddy, would you love Norma-mom if I wasn't here?"

Teddy stared at him. "Are you going away, Dad?"

[114]

Ben sighed. "I might."

"But I don't want you to go!" Teddy's eyes filled with tears.

"Don't want to go, either."

Teddy wiped at his face with one hand. "Can I come with you?"

Ben smiled again and reached for Teddy's other hand. "Don't cry, son." He took a deep breath. "Can't come this time. Need you and Daniel to . . . look after Norma-mom."

Teddy thought about that for a few moments. "Can't we all go?" he sniffed.

"'Fraid not, son. Have to go myself."

"How long will you be gone?"

"Long time. Long, long time."

"Well then, we'll wait for you. We'll take care of Norma-mom and wait for you."

"That's my boy." Ben tightened his grip on the small hand.

Norma came into the room. "How was the story?"

Ben smiled up at her. "Good."

Teddy wiped his eyes. "Dad liked it, Norma-mom! And guess what! Daniel and I are going to take care of you!" He slid off the bed, wrapped his arms around her legs and squeezed hard, then flew out of the room.

Norma moved closer to the bed and looked down at Ben. "Are you giving up on me, Mr. Frosst?" she demanded, the blue eyes pooling with tears.

Ben smiled. "Never giving up." Then he sighed. "Just . . . being prepared."

Norma climbed up on the bed beside him and curled against his side. "Oh, Ben." She reached for his hand.

His fingers tightened over hers. "I love you Norma. So much."

"I love you, Ben. More than you'll ever know."

Chapter Ten

Rob and Harriett came into the living room. "It's time, Norma,"
Rob said. "The cars are here."

Norma looked up from the tie she was tying around Daniel's
throat. "We're almost ready, Rob."

Daniel reached out a hand and cupped Norma's cheek. "Don't be
sad, Norma-mom."

Norma patted his hand, then ducked her head and reached for a
handkerchief. "It's hard not to be, son."

"But you know he's happy."

"It's one thing to *know*," Norma blew her nose, "And another
thing to *accept*."

Daniel frowned slightly, digesting this.

Teddy came into the room. "Norma-mom! There's a big, long car
in the driveway!"

Norma smiled slightly. "Yes. Isn't it a beautiful car?"

"The driver let me sit in the front seat and showed me all of the
neat stuff. The radio has big, shiny knobs and he let me twist them.
There are big, white tires and a flying lady on the very front!"

"A flying lady! That is exciting!"

Teddy nodded. "Anyway, he says to tell you that it's time."

"Yes, son, I know." Norma sighed. "Time to go." She turned toward the door, then started slightly when someone linked their arm through hers. She glanced over at Daniel's set face.

"Told Dad we'd look after you, Norma-mom. We will."

Teddy took her other arm and the three of them left the room.

* * *

A few hours later, Norma, with a boy on each side of her, stood at the outer door of the house saying farewell to a long line of people. "Thank you, yes; the service was lovely." She shook yet another hand.

Slowly, the people moved out into the street and either walked quickly away, or slid into their nearby automobiles.

Norma watched them go. "It was nice to see how many people loved him," she said, dabbing at her eyes with her handkerchief.

"Everyone does," Daniel said. "Everyone."

Another person stopped in the doorway and offered her his hand. "Lovely ceremony, Norma."

"Yes it was. Thank you so much for being here."

The man looked around. "Wouldn't have missed it. Ben did so much for us. It's the least we could do for him."

Norma nodded and summoned up a smile.

The man clapped his hat on his head and turned away.

"Look! Norma-mom! There's a robin!"

Norma followed Teddy's pointing finger. Sure enough, a robin was hopping along the brown grass beside the walk where the snow had receded.

"Looks like spring," she said.

Daniel sighed. "Dad loved winter so much."

Norma nodded. "It was his favourite time."

"Norma-mom, what's that?"

Norma turned and again followed Teddy's eagerly pointing finger.

"Why, I don't know, son."

Someone had rolled up a ball of snow, then another and another and stacked them atop one another, largest to smallest. The top ball had been fitted with a couple of pieces of black coal, a carrot and more pieces of coal. They seemed to form a sort of face with eyes, a nose and a smiling mouth. Several small pieces of coal trailed down

[119]

the front, obviously forming buttons. The figure had been warmly wrapped in a long, knitted scarf and topped off with a battered silk top hat.

Norma frowned. "It looks like a man. A snow man."

"Like Dad," Teddy said. "He was a snow man."

Norma froze. That was what it was! A legless man made out of snow.

Daniel pointed. "Look. He's smiling!"

Norma nodded and smiled herself. It was exactly as Ben should be.

"Look. There's another one!" Teddy said excitedly.

Norma turned to see that a second snow man had been constructed near the entrance to the yard.

"And two more!" Daniel pointed.

Teddy grabbed her arm and tried to tow her out into the yard. "They're everywhere, Norma-mom!"

Norma scanned the yard, counting. Eight, ten. There must have been a dozen of the little figures.

Daniel smiled. "Everyone is remembering Dad. Frosty. Our town's Snow Man."

[120]

Epilogue

The mayor braced booted feet in the deep snow, clasped gloved hands behind him and looked over the field fondly, taking in the rows of snowmen surrounding the large park and the groups of Broomball players racing up and down the smooth, snowy surface, intent on their respective games. "Yes, over the past 75-plus years, it's become quite a tradition in our little town," he said.

The young man beside him lowered his camera. "But, Mr. Mayor, why the snowmen? I mean, I can understand about the annual Broomball tournament, but why the Snowman-building competition?"

The mayor frowned. "No one really knows. Well, maybe if you could find some of the old-timers who were around when the whole thing started back in the early 1940s."

"Well, you said it, sir. That's nearly 75 years ago now. Not many of them left anymore."

The Mayor nodded. "None that I know. At least none clear enough to remember much of anything." He sighed and turned his head, then pointed to the west. "I know that the people who used to live in the old Frosst home, over that way, had something to do with

[121]

it. But the old couple died, as did one of their sons on Okinawa during the war. The remaining boy could probably have told you, but he never married and is long gone now." He shook his head. "No, I guess the origin of our tradition is pretty much lost now."

"Well, there's still the song."

"Frosty, the Snowman?" The Mayor smiled. "Oh, I think that was just written for the festival. I don't think there's any actual history."

"Yeah. A snowman running around in a top hat and waving a broomstick." The young man laughed. "Hardly believable!"

The Mayor laughed. "As you say." He reached out a hand. "Well, thank you for visiting our little town, young man. Glad you could make it."

"I've always been meaning to stop here." The young man shook the proffered hand, then lifted his camera and snapped another picture. "Just sorry it took me so long. This is quite a spectacle!"

"Yes. We do things up rather well, don't we?" The Mayor laughed and glanced again across the huge playing field. "Oh, look! They're about to start the parade. Would you care to join us? Everyone's invited."

[122]

The young man followed the Mayor's gaze. "Looks like fun. Lead on!"

The two of them started across the field.

The young man snapped a couple of pictures of snowmen as he and the mayor walked past. One was carved entirely out of blue snow and the other dressed in a style faintly reminiscent of the 'hippie era'. "So, how many snowmen were there in the competition this year?"

The mayor smiled proudly. "I think we had over 500 entries this year. Best year ever!"

"So, between the Broomball attracting thousands and the snowman competition attracting thousands more, your little town must be bursting at the seams!"

The Mayor smiled. "Yes, we are. But only for a week out of the year. The rest of the time, the tourist traffic is a bit more manageable."

The young man was silent for a moment. "So . . . no history."

"Beg your pardon?"

"Nothing. Just talking to myself."

"Well, better not make a habit of it."

[123]

The young man stopped and looked around. "Don't you think it's rather amazing that all of this started somewhere and no one knows how? There had to have been a first time. I mean *someone* must have started the broomball tournament. *Someone* must have come up with the idea of the snowman competition."

The Mayor stopped beside him. "Never really thought about it."

"Here is this great story . . ."

"You're imagining that it's great," the Mayor put in.

"Well . . . yes, I guess I am. Anyway, this great story hidden in the mists of time that, for the past 75 years has caused your town to, once a year, become one of the busiest, happiest places on earth. I mean - surely the tourist dollars alone that this festival brings in . . ."

"Where are you trying to go with this?"

"Well, I guess it just seems such a shame that this amazing story has been reduced to a tournament, a song and a joyfully-smiling effigy."

The Mayor smiled. "But the important part is still here. The joy."

The young man looked thoughtful as he started walking again. Finally, he nodded. "Yeah." He smiled as he lifted his camera. "The joy."

[124]

Diane Stringam Tolley was born and raised on the great Alberta prairies. Daughter of a ranching family of writers, she inherited her love of writing at a very early age. Trained in Journalism, she has penned countless articles and short stories. She is the published author of five e-books and the Christmas novels, Carving Angels and (Kris Kringle's) Magic by Cedar Fort Publishing as well as a book of poetry. She and her husband, Grant, live in Beaumont, Alberta, and are the parents of six children and grandparents of thirteen-plus.

Email: dtolley@shaw.ca

Facebook : http://facebook.com/diane.tolley1

Twitter: http://twitter.com/StoryTolley

Web Site: www.dianestringamtolley.com

Blog: www.dlt-lifeontheranch.blogspot.com

Video: https://vimeo.com/45744176

Podcast: http://www.practicalpodcasting.com/kris-kringles-magic-diane-stringam-tolley-author/

Made in the USA
Charleston, SC
04 December 2015